BLOODIER THAN FICTION

A Bookish Cafe Mystery Book 2

HARPER LIN

This is a work of fiction. Names, characters, organizations, places, events, and incidents are either products of the author's imagination or are used fictitiously.

Bloodier Than Fiction

ISBN: 978-1-987859-86-7

www.harperlin.com

Chapter 1

The new shipments of books mocked Maggie Bell. There were three cardboard boxes of the latest football-themed novels and biographies, all to celebrate the Fair Haven High School football team playing their last home game of an undefeated season. Visitors had been trickling in even though the home game wasn't for another three weeks. Business had been booming. People were stopping in the café and finding their way into the bookstore in a steady stream for days. All of them asking her the same question. Would she be attending the game?

"I'll probably have to work" was her usual reply before she pushed her glasses up higher, to which they'd gasp and shake their heads and frown.

"Oh, that's too bad," they'd gush. "Maybe your boss will let you out early to catch the second half."

"I hope not," she'd quietly reply, which got even more critical looks.

It was bad enough the display window was bursting with pom-poms, flags, and footballs alongside the classic sports books she'd plucked from the shelves and carefully arranged. Maggie had no idea what constituted a good sports book. It was a topic she'd avoided simply because she never watched any games. It was like every customer who came in over the past couple of days was speaking another language, and she just couldn't gather even the slightest hint as to what they were talking about. They knew the names of players, the positions they played, the records of the other teams they already defeated, and who was coming up. Maggie knew the Fair Haven team were called the Bulldogs and their colors were red and blue. That was the extent of her knowledge on the team.

However, what she lacked in smarts when it came to the sport she made up for in the display window that featured not just football titles but *How to Raise and Train Your Bulldog, Zelda Wisdom, and English Bulldogs for Dummies.* The customers seemed to enjoy it. Secretly, Maggie thought it was rather clever on her part too. But she couldn't help still miss the old days when her friend and the owner of the store was still alive.

The Bookish Café, formerly called Whitfield Book Shop, had been a dusty, antiquated bookstore that rarely had a visitor. To Maggie, it was as comfortable as a warm quilt. Now it was becoming a trendy hot spot for visitors and locals alike. Maggie missed the days of sitting at the counter, reading something by Dumas or Hugo uninterrupted with Poe, the bookshop cat, purring pleasantly next to her. Poe didn't seem to mind the increase in traffic through the store as it usually meant an extra couple of scratches behind the ears.

After a deep breath, Maggie wrinkled her nose at the boxes and reached over to the old desk where Mr. Alexander Whitfield had spent so many days chatting with her before his death. A pair of ornate scissors, razor-sharp, lay there. Maggie grabbed them and split the seams of the boxes with hesitation, as if their contents smelled foul.

There were some interesting books inside about people whose names she recognized, like Joe Namath and Peyton Manning. They'd been in the news or something, she thought. But all the rest looked the same. Men in helmets, carrying a ball under their arms with huge, padded shoulders and thighs, running or falling or posing like jersey-clad male supermodels. Most of the books were described as the stories of courage or perseverance or courageous perseverance that resulted in a Heisman Trophy or a Super Bowl ring.

"See anything you like?" Joshua Whitfield asked with a smirk.

"I don't get it," Maggie replied. "All this hoopla for a *game*. Have you seen Tammy's bakery? You'd think a red-and-blue fabric store threw up in there."

Tammy McCarthy's bakery was just down the street. It was a wonderful place that made the entire block smell of cinnamon, which was especially nice at this time of the year, when the mornings were crisp with hints of fall. Maggie was there every morning to pick up pastries to bring to the café. It was a wonderful business move that Joshua had established as soon as he took over the bookstore and built the café.

"Are you kidding?" Joshua asked, looking at Maggie as if she'd suddenly sprouted antennas. "It's not just a game. It's man at his most aggressive in the continual quest not only for goals but for glory."

Maggie stared at Joshua, blinking like a deer in

the headlights. Joshua walked up to her and put his arm around her shoulder.

"Just imagine being in the stands of a stadium, looking down on a rectangular field, with one team on one side and their rival on the other. They face off in formation. Talking smack as the play is called. The snap! The ball is thrown down the field. Does he catch it? Is it intercepted? Does he make the yards, or is he tackled? It's anybody's guess. And that's where the thrill is. The crowd shouts. The smell of hot dogs and nachos and popcorn fills the air. Hot chocolate keeps your hands toasty. The sun beats down on your face. You can't beat it. At least not until baseball season starts."

"Lord help us." Maggie huffed. The truth was she could have stood there for hours with Joshua's arm around her. He wore an intoxicating aftershave that reminded her of oranges and clove cigarettes. But she didn't dare let him think she had such thoughts.

"Oh, come on Mags." Joshua chuckled as he pulled his arm away and took a few steps back to watch her return to the boxes of books.

"I'll pass. And I don't mean with a football." She pulled out a few more books, looked at them like they were covered in fungus, and set them down in stacks.

Joshua laughed. "Have you ever been to a game?"

"No," she replied without looking up.

"Never? Oh no. That just won't do. We've got the high school game coming up. I am making it mandatory for all my employees to attend," Joshua said.

"Well, since that's just me, I say no," Maggie replied.

"Oh no. I've got people coming in to interview for the two jobs that opened up," Joshua said as he headed over to the cubby he'd been working on to house the more valuable books for sale. There were a few that his father had collected that weren't worth as much as the books he'd left to Maggie in his will but were still a good investment for a beginner collector.

"What did you say?" Maggie choked.

"I need someone to help behind the counter. Tammy's got too much on her plate as it is. She can't keep pitching in over here. So I put an ad in the paper and got a couple replies. They'll be coming in throughout the day," Joshua said. "I'd appreciate your help if they come in the bookstore.

Just tell them to have a seat in the café," Joshua said as he held a level on the shelves one last time before he started to attach the decorative glass door with the skeleton key lock on it.

"Well, the café has gotten pretty busy." Maggie swallowed after speaking.

"Yeah, and so has the bookstore. I've seen you running back when the deliveries come just to run up front to ring up a sale or answer a question. So I'm also looking for a stock boy to help both of us," Joshua said without looking up from his work.

"I really don't need anyone to help me," Maggie insisted while nodding her head. "You can save yourself the extra money. I'm good."

"Too late," Joshua replied. "They'll be coming in throughout the day."

"What if I don't like any of the candidates? They should have a basic understanding of the kinds of books we have and be familiar with all the classics, plus some of the more obscure titles for our more discerning customers and…"

"You aren't interviewing any of them. I am. I'll decide who will be competent enough to help with stocking the shelves," Joshua replied with a smirk.

"You didn't even ask me if I wanted any help,"

Maggie replied, and her hands automatically went to her hips.

"You would have told me you didn't need any help." Joshua went back to the bookshelf.

"I don't think I like this."

"All the more reason to do it," Joshua teased as he turned around and stepped aside for her to see the bookshelf was just about done. "We just need to varnish the wood. I'll have your new assistant do it. Did I tell you that you'll get to tell them what to do too?"

"I will?" Maggie said.

"You can't go crazy. You're not Captain Queeg. At least I hope not," Joshua said.

The reference to *The Caine Mutiny's* captain made her burst out laughing. Quickly, she regained her composure, nervously tugging on the hem and cuffs of her sweater before turning around to get back to the football books she had been unpacking.

At first, she felt itchy and uncomfortable in her own skin as the thought of new people infiltrating her sanctuary came into focus. But what Joshua had said was true. The foot traffic had increased, and sales were better than she'd ever seen them. Although people were buying more of the drivel that was on the New York Times Best Sellers list rather than really diving in deep to the classics, at least they were reading. And that, her friend Alexander Whitfield would say, made it all worth it.

Still, she was hesitant just to accept the people Joshua decided to hire. If they were going to work in the bookstore at all, they would have to have some kinds of qualifications. Maybe a degree in literature or library sciences. They would at least have to be well read, having knowledge of the major authors throughout history and some, or very few, of the more contemporary authors. Perhaps she could quickly draw up a couple of questions and give those to Joshua to help him screen out the riffraff.

She grabbed a pad of paper and a pen and placed it next to the boxes she was emptying. As an interview question came to mind, she'd quickly scribble it down. By the time she'd finished pulling out all the books, organizing them, and finally placing them either in her display or on the shelves, she had over twenty-five questions for Joshua to ask the interviewee who would eventually be working with her. Just as she was about to present them to him, the bells over the door jingled, and a wafer-thin girl with green hair tied neatly in a bun and combat boots walked into the bookshop.

Chapter 2

"Can I help you?" Maggie asked, wondering when this look came back in style.

"Yeah, I'm here to see Joshua Whitfield about a job," she replied politely. Maggie did as she had been instructed and told the young lady to take a seat in the café. She then took her list of questions and walked up to Joshua, who was busy in the back room of the café, measuring a big space against the far wall.

"What's going to go there?" Maggie asked.

"An oven, if I can figure out how to route the gas," he replied before wiping a little sweat from his brow. He looked so ruggedly handsome Maggie almost forgot what she was there for. After clearing her throat, she looked down at the piece of paper in her hands and shook her head.

"There's a girl with green hair here to see you," Maggie said. "And here." She handed over the piece of paper that Joshua squinted at before focusing and reading the words.

"What is this?"

"Just some questions to ask the person who is going to be primarily helping me." Maggie shrugged. "They aren't hard questions. It's just to gauge where they are when it comes to literature. That's all."

"What was the primary drive of popular eighteenth-century authors in the area of domestic life? Are you serious?" Joshua laughed and shook his head before handing the sheet of paper back to Maggie.

"You aren't going to hire someone for the café who doesn't know the difference between a croissant and a scone, are you?" Maggie huffed.

"Even if they didn't know the difference, Maggie, I think they'd learn it by, oh, say, the end of their first day. This isn't rocket science. Look, I know you take your job seriously, but I just need some people to help. You are going to have to trust me that I know what I'm doing," Joshua said before he took a small notebook from his back pocket and flipped it open. "The girl you are talking about must be Zoey. Well, she's on time. That's a good start, don't you think?"

Maggie rolled her eyes as Joshua scooted past her and went out into the café to begin what already felt like a grueling process.

With her head held high, Maggie followed Joshua and slipped back into the bookstore without making any eye contact with *Zoey*. With the boxes of books nearly empty, she had enough to do to keep herself occupied. But the fact that Joshua wouldn't even allow her to have a say in the people he was going to invite into his late father's store ruffled her feathers.

After about twenty minutes, Zoey left the store with a smile on her face. She didn't wave or say anything to Maggie on her way out, and Maggie was just fine with that. The temptation to go ask Joshua what his impression of the green-haired beauty was nagged at her, but she was afraid to hear his answer.

"She's wonderful" or "She's perfect" or "She's just the kind of edginess the bookstore and café need" were phrases she dreaded hearing. That girl belonged at one of those chain coffee shops where the people at the counter cracked jokes and put on skits while trying to make some made-up coffee drink no one ever heard of. So she remained in the bookstore, acting as if she didn't care what Joshua ultimately did.

After about ten minutes, another person came into the bookstore looking for Joshua. She was dressed to the hilt in a nice pantsuit, and Maggie wondered if she knew she *might* get dirty working in the café and the bookstore.

"I have an interview with him for café administrator." She pronounced her words perfectly and towered over Maggie by at least a foot.

"Have a seat in the café. I'll get him for you," Maggie said as professionally as she could muster. Inside she was laughing. A café administrator? After Joshua took a seat and began to explain the job, Mrs. Administrator stood up, shook her head, and stomped out. Joshua looked at Maggie and shrugged while chuckling. It was contagious, and Maggie did the same thing.

The third person was a tall, wiry young man who looked like he was as nervous as a dog on the Fourth of July.

"I'm here to see Joshua about a stock boy job," he said to Maggie.

"Just have a seat," she said and pointed to the small table for two in the corner that Joshua had reserved for his interviews.

On his way to the café side of the store, the young man stopped and picked up one of the books that was being displaced for the football-themed inventory. It was a small vintage hardcover of *Black Buggy* by some author Maggie couldn't place at the moment. She'd read the book years ago and remembered liking it as a novel about the days preceding the Civil War. She watched him open it to the first pages and begin to read. Within a few seconds, he closed the book, looked at the price tag, and then carefully put it back where he'd found it.

Joshua saw him and quickly came to the table. They talked at length. Before Maggie could ask, the young man was shaking Joshua's hand with a bit of a frown on his face and left the shop quickly.

He was who Maggie wanted to stock the shelves. It was obvious that he read or at least knew how to read, which was more than she could say for Zoey-green-hair and Mrs. Administrator.

But Joshua assured her he had people scheduled to come in all day. And so they did. There were mostly women who wanted to work in the café. More than one of them bragged about watching the cooking competitions and had dreams of creating masterpiece cupcakes and pies. Maggie didn't think there was anything wrong with that except for the fact that Joshua needed someone to run the register and clean the place, and there wasn't even an oven set up in the back yet. What kind of ad had he placed in the paper that these people were expecting so much from The Bookish Café?

A couple hours later, Maggie had encountered three more candidates, and each one of them was more interested in making goo-goo eyes at Joshua than learning what their job description was going to be. At least that was how it looked to Maggie. One man who came in, wearing a tie and sport coat, seemed very nice until Joshua had to step away from the table for just a minute. That was when Maggie saw the clean-cut man pick his nose and wipe his hand under the café table. If he did that, there was no telling what he'd be doing around the food. She made a note of it and would tell Joshua after the man left.

There was another woman who brought a stack of papers and was constantly shuffling through them, handing them to Joshua just to take them back and give him another one. It was like a two-

person game of *Button. Button. Who's got the button.*
Except every time Joshua had the "button," the
woman snatched it away and replaced it with
another.

Maggie would have found it funny to watch if
the woman's disheveled appearance and unorganized manner didn't rub against the grain. Maggie
didn't want an unorganized, discombobulated
person messing with her bookstore. Sure, it was
technically Joshua's bookstore, but Maggie tended
to it. She knew where everything was at, how it was
organized, and what things could be moved where.
It wasn't just some sloppy thrift store with a couple
of random bookcases filled with discarded cook-
books and self-help tutorials. This was a real bookstore. The kind that was hard to find nowadays.

Finally, near the end of the day, a big, burly guy
who looked like he should be chopping down trees
in a forest came into the bookstore. He looked
around, smiled at Maggie and, in a soft voice, said
hello.

"Is there a Joshua Whitfield who works here?"
he asked.

"Yes, are you here for the interview?" Maggie
asked.

"No, my wife is. But she is busy nursing our new

baby in the car. It will only take her a minute. I just wanted to let Mr. Whitfield know she wasn't late, but our boy eats whenever he decides he's hungry." He smiled, and it was contagious. Maggie smiled back and told him she'd tell Joshua that she'd be in as soon as she was finished. It was obvious that this was a very proud papa. He thanked Maggie and hurried back outside.

"She's nursing?" Joshua scratched his head. "That might interfere with her time here."

"I don't know about that. I find the whole ritual a little off-putting. But she was considerate enough to send her husband in to say she'd be just a few minutes. That's considerate, I guess," Maggie insisted and shrugged at the same time. "What do I know about the etiquette of mothers with new babies?"

Joshua looked down at her and squinted his eyes. "Not much."

"Well, if you are leaning toward Mr. Clean-cut in the sports jacket, I've got a little information to tell you that ought to scare him right off your list."

"I did like him. He was my first choice. What is it?"

"I'll tell you after you talk to this lady," Maggie said. After a few minutes, a full-figured blonde with bright-red lips and red gym shoes came into the store, tugging at her bra strap and trying to smooth her shirt down.

"Hi, I'm here to see Joshua about a job." She panted as if she had sprinted from six blocks away. Maggie told her to take a seat, and as with her husband, there was just something likable about her. And Maggie knew herself to know that she didn't really like anyone.

"My name is Barbara Whels, but everyone calls me Babs. What's your name?" Babs said and extended her hand to Maggie, who couldn't help but notice the bright-red polish on her fingers.

"Margaret. But everyone calls me Maggie," she replied, unaware that she was smiling. Maggie wasn't used to smiling so easily at anyone who came into the bookstore and almost had to catch herself and replace her grin with her signature squinty look.

"Thanks for giving me a few extra minutes. My husband is a nervous new father. He wanted me to feed our son before I left in case the interview went long. I said to him this isn't like I'm interviewing for the CIA. It's a café, for heaven's sake." She laughed a deep chuckle.

"Well, you can have a seat, and Joshua will be

with you in a few minutes." Maggie hurried the conversation along for fear she might enjoy chatting too much.

As it turned out, Babs seemed to have the same effect on Joshua, as they chatted easily and comfortably for a while before she stood up, shook his hand, and proceeded to leave.

"It was nice meeting you, Maggie." She waved as she left the bookstore.

"You too, Babs." Maggie waved as best she could with her arms full of books.

Joshua appeared and looked at his watch. "You were right. She was really nice, and I think probably a little overqualified."

"Are you going to hire her?" Maggie asked, trying not to sound too interested.

"I am," he replied, waiting for her smile of approval. Instead, he got a harumph and head shaking. "What's wrong?"

"A new baby? A nervous father? I don't know," Maggie replied. She didn't want Joshua to know that she secretly had chosen the same people as he did.

"And I'm going to hire Casper Lahey as our stock boy and gopher. He seems like a good kid and has his head on straight," Joshua said, raising his chin.

"How old is he?" Maggie asked.

"Nineteen. Why?" Joshua asked. Maggie didn't want to tell him that he was who she'd thought was the best choice, too, based on the fact he picked up one of the books she liked. The last thing she wanted to admit was that she agreed with him, especially after he dismissed her line of questioning for the potential candidates.

"Nineteen-year-olds can be irresponsible some-times," she added. It was the truth.

"I don't think we are going to have that problem with Casper. Something in my gut tells me he's a good egg," Joshua replied.

Maggie shrugged and went back to her work. If she let on she was happy with his choices, he'd tease her about not just her line of questioning he'd so easily tossed aside but also about their mutual desire for the same people to work with them. It was infu-riating that she'd have anything in common with him, no matter how good he smelled or how hand-some he was when he stood close, looking down at her with those twinkling eyes.

After what only felt like a few minutes, when Maggie looked at the clock, she couldn't believe it was almost quitting time. The day had flown by, and still, the window display wasn't completed, and another shipment of books arrived that hadn't been unpacked.

There were stacks of old books that needed to be boxed up and were going to find their way to Broken Hill State Penitentiary. Maggie had done a little research and found out they had a library. She asked if instead of sending the old books or over-stocks to the local thrift stores if they could donate them to the prison. It might not have been proper, but Maggie enjoyed the thought of some of those big burly inmates reading copies of *Lady Chatterley's Lover* or *The Tropic of Cancer*.

"It's better than having them lift weights," Joshua joked. Maggie didn't laugh.

"Well, if Casper is supposed to help with the heavy lifting, I'll let him take those to the post office," Maggie said to Poe, who had finally hopped up on the counter to occupy a square of sunshine. He purred and butted his head against hers when she leaned forward. All Maggie hoped was that Casper was as quiet in the bookstore as he seemed in his interview.

Chapter 3

"You're sure you are okay?" Mr. Whels said as he escorted Babs into the café with a beautiful, bald, round-headed baby strapped to his big barrel chest.

"Roy, I'm fine. Honey, please," Babs said as she stroked the huge man's beard.

"If you need me, just call. We're only ten minutes away," Roy said. He'd said the same thing to her every day since she'd started working four days ago.

"I know. You take care of Daddy, Earl. Be a good boy," she said to the baby as she gently rubbed his bald head and kissed his chubby cheeks. Every day she did that, too, and every day it made Maggie smile and quickly turn away. Gushing over a baby was not her style.

Babs had turned out to be better than either Joshua or Maggie could have expected. Not only was she great with customers, but she knew quite a bit about electrical work, carpentry, and cooking. She made all her baby's clothes by hand and had helped Roy build a tree house with two sleeping rooms and a staircase for when the little tike got older.

"I was homeschooled." She chuckled. "One of the drawbacks of being homeschooled is that you learn how to do more for yourself, so you never have a spare minute to relax. There is always something that needs to be done."

"Maggie, do you want me to dust those top shelves like you'd mentioned yesterday?" Casper had sidled up to her as she was watching Babs and Roy perform their morning ritual. His voice was always soft and apologetic. Like he was sorry for having to speak at all. Maggie liked him.

"Yes, if you would. And after that, I wanted to try to condense some of popular topics that we now have more room for since we donated all those books," she replied.

"Why do you send those books to the prison?" Casper asked.

Maggie looked up at him and scrunched up her nose. "Just because they are convicts doesn't mean they shouldn't have a chance to read a good book."

The corners of Casper's lips curled up just slightly before he nodded and went back to work. For the past few days, he'd done exactly as he was told. On his breaks, Maggie caught him perusing the titles on the shelves and pulling out a few that he would quickly scan before putting back. She had told him he could take any book and read it at his leisure so long as he brought it back when he was done.

"I might just do that," he said softly.

Maggie tried to get to know him a little, but her questions sounded more like an interrogation than friendly chatter.

"Where did you go to school?"

"How long have you lived here?"

"What other jobs have you worked? Where? In what capacity?"

Finally, she stopped since most of his answers were just a few words before he'd pull up his shoulders and continue with the work at hand.

Most of the talk that took place in the café was

about the football game. Babs was a regular cornucopia of football trivia. She was as excited as the kids who were playing.

"An undefeated season is a huge accomplishment. Those kids are under a lot of pressure. No one would be disappointed if they didn't pull it off. But it sure is exciting," Babs would go on with any customers that came in. They were just as enthralled as she was. Why not? It was the most exciting thing to happen in Fair Haven since the flood that had knocked out the bridges and kept everyone stranded here for days several months back.

"Are you going to the football game?" Maggie asked Casper when they were alone and she was tallying receipts from the day before.

"No. I don't like sports" was all he said before walking away.

Once again, he got another check in the "good" column Maggie was keeping in her mind. She wanted to ask him what he and his friends did if they weren't into sports, but she was afraid it would look like she was prying. Over the past few days, she'd noticed a couple kids who waited outside and across the street for Casper when he left. As soon as he appeared, they usually jogged off after him. It wasn't until Maggie was putting the finishing touches on the display window did she realize there was a real problem with the boys who waited every day for Casper.

"Do you need me for anything else?" Casper asked before he left every day since he started. His voice was always soft as he stood, like he was a private waiting for instructions from his sergeant.

"No. I'm just putting some finishing touches on the window, and then I'll be leaving myself," Maggie said.

As much as she tried to be friendly, it was just too awkward, like she was trying to whistle after eating a stack of crackers. Socializing with strangers was not in her repertoire. There were too many opportunities for the whole exchange to go sideways. Even though Casper wasn't a stranger anymore, he was as quiet and into his own head as Maggie was. They roamed the aisles of the bookstore, completing their tasks as they popped up with almost no words exchanged between them. It was the perfect arrangement.

But on this particular evening, as Casper put his lightweight jacket on and went to leave for the day, Maggie followed him outside to look at the display window from a pedestrian's point of view. That was when she realized the two boys that had been waiting for Casper were not friends.

"Casper!" one shouted as they both jogged across the street to catch up to him. They didn't dress like Casper, who was just a tall, skinny kid who wore a black T-shirt every day, tucked neatly into the waistband of his jeans, and black boots. His hair was a little long and had a natural wave in it that caused him to flip his head to get it away from hanging in his face. But these boys who came up to him looked a lot different upon close inspection.

"Where you goin'?" the other boy asked as he stood in front of Casper. He was wearing a rust-colored hoodie with the hood pulled over a white baseball cap. His eyes were set far apart, and his mouth was nothing more than a thin slit in his face. Maggie watched as Casper looked down at the sidewalk and then across the street as if he were searching for someone and not hearing the two boys who had crossed his path. The second boy tapped Casper on the shoulder to get his attention. He was stockier than the other two with the physique of a bulldog, heavy at the shoulders and chest then tapering off around the waist and legs. His neck was thick, and his hair looked like someone had put a bowl on it and cut around the edges. He could have been part of her display for the Fair Haven High School team.

"I told you guys I'm not interested," Casper said in his soft way.

"That doesn't matter, Casper. We're interested in you," the bulldog said.

Maggie watched out of the corner of her eye as they muscled Casper up against the wall. There were very few people out, and those that were paid no attention to what the three young men were doing. For anyone passing by, they looked like nothing more than some friends talking. But Maggie could tell by Casper's mannerisms that he was not friends with these people.

They muttered and spoke firmly to him, but she couldn't make out what they were saying. Then, out of the blue, the scrawny fellow in the white baseball cap slapped Casper across the face. Maggie's chest tightened. Part of her wanted to rush up and get between Casper and the two boys, but she didn't. Not only might it have embarrassed him, but there was also a danger factor. Just as she was contemplating what to do, Casper pushed the boy who slapped him and took a brave step forward. It was two against one.

As they stood toe-to-toe, Maggie had an idea.

Without giving herself time to think through her plan, she called Casper's name.

"Casper! Thank goodness you are still here! I need you for one last thing!" She shouted and waved at him as if she hadn't seen anything that had just happened.

The two boys stepped aside and let Casper pass. His cheeks were bright red, and he stomped away from them without looking back.

"I'm sorry to interrupt," Maggie said with a crooked smile. "I needed two of the books on that top shelf down because I've got someone coming in tomorrow who wants to take a look at them. I forgot all about it. But even on tiptoes, I can't reach," she lied.

Together, they walked to the back of the store where the bookshelves went almost to the ceiling. Thinking quickly, Maggie pointed to one huge tome of drawn illustrations of fish of the Amazon and then quickly spied another that was *The Derby Special.* It was a book she'd never read. But it looked old, and now that it was coming down off the shelf and the dust was being blown off it, she thought she just might.

"Thanks, Casper. You can go ahead with your friends now," she said and watched his face. He mumbled something before he turned and walked toward the door.

After waiting a few seconds, Maggie hurried on the tips of her toes to the door, opened it, and peeked around the corner. Casper was alone on the sidewalk, heading home. She scanned the street for the other two boys but didn't see them. Her breath that she hadn't realized she was holding came out in a long sigh of relief.

Young men Casper's age usually didn't want interference from adults in their affairs. But it picked at Maggie as to whether or not she should tell Joshua about what she saw. It was difficult, but she decided not to do anything. Casper pushed back. Those boys might have realized he was not a pushover, and this would be the end of things. With that her only comforting thought about the whole situation, she grabbed her bag and keys, locked up the bookstore side of the storefront, and left for the evening.

Chapter 4

"There are three streets blocked off!" Maggie burst into the café to find Joshua and Babs standing behind the counter. They stared at her like she had sprouted one antler out of the middle of her forehead.

"Yeah, they are getting ready for the game coming up next week," Babs said.

"I had to practically park on the other side of town. And this is going to be like this for how long?" Maggie huffed.

"From now until the game, I guess," Joshua added. It wasn't the answer Maggie wanted to hear. She threw her arms up, let out a grunt, and stomped into the bookstore side of the building.

"I just love her," Babs said. "She's like a cartoon character."

"She's a character, all right," Joshua replied. Maggie heard the exchange and blushed. She didn't mind what Babs had said. It wasn't a lie. But the fact that Joshua chimed in with his own opinion made a wave of heat rush over her skin.

"Whatever," she muttered and went to unlock the front door. No sooner had she snapped the dead bolt back did Casper come bursting into the shop. He pushed past Maggie, almost knocking her off her feet.

"Sorry," he huffed, barely looking at her as he hurried to the back of the bookstore.

The first thing Maggie noticed was that his shirt and jeans were dirty, like he'd fallen to the ground. His hair was mussed, and his hands looked red and scraped.

"Casper?" Maggie called then looked toward the café then back at Casper. He turned around. His face was scratched, and there was a small shiner developing under his left eye.

Maggie pinched her lips together, looked again into the café where Joshua and Babs were still talking, then—feeling Casper and she were safe from any interruptions—hurried up to him.

"What happened to you?" she whispered.

"It's nothing, Maggie. I'm fine," he said with clenched teeth.

Maggie looked up at him. Even though he was only nineteen, he towered over her.

"Why don't you go in the bathroom and wash up?" she said. "I'll grab some ice from the café, and you can put that on your eye."

"Please don't tell Joshua," he pleaded. "I promise it won't happen again."

Maggie took a deep breath and patted Casper's arm awkwardly but gently. "Don't worry. I won't say anything. But in order for me to help you, you and I are going to have to have a talk. Okay?"

With his shoulders almost up to his ears, Casper nodded and went in the bathroom, shutting the door behind him. Maggie could hear the water running before she went to the café for some ice.

"What is that for?" Joshua asked as he watched her take a small scoop from behind the counter and dump the ice into a small paper cup.

"I thought I'd have iced coffee this morning. If you must know," Maggie replied, bugging her eyes, annoyed at his inquiry.

Joshua squinted at Maggie as she scooted past him.

"Good morning, Babs. How's the baby?" Maggie asked, still keeping her eyes on Joshua.

"Oh, Earl is just fine, thanks for asking," Babs replied with a grin. "If only Roy would relax."

Joshua chuckled. Before any more could be said, she squeezed past Joshua with her ice in a cup and headed back to the bookstore. For a second, she thought of stopping and asking what they planned on doing throughout the course of the day in order to keep them at bay so Casper could lick his wounds in a semi-private atmosphere. But she thought that might look too suspicious. So she kept her mouth shut and just hurried into the back of the bookstore.

In Mr. Whitfield's desk, Maggie knew she'd find an old kerchief of his. He was not one for Kleenex, as he hated how he had the tendency to forget it in his pockets and then toss the clothes in the wash. By the time he pulled it from the dryer, there was shredded tissue everywhere. So cloth handkerchiefs were all he used, and he kept them on hand. With one of them tucked into the cup, its initials A.W. peeking over the top, Maggie softly rapped on the bathroom door. Casper came out looking better with his hands cleaned and his hair smoothed out and his face washed. Maggie couldn't be sure, but she thought he might have been crying. Who could blame him?

"Are you all right?" she asked.

"Yes." He sniffed as she handed him the kerchief and cup of ice.

He dumped the ice into the white cloth, folded it over on itself, and applied it to the bump under his eye.

"Do you want to talk about it?" Maggie asked, wrinkling her nose.

"No," Casper said.

"Is there anything I can do?"

"Don't worry about it," Casper replied. "I've got it under control."

"Does this have anything to do with the kids I saw you with yesterday?" Maggie tilted her head and looked at Casper with squinted eyes.

"Really, Maggie. Don't worry about it. I don't want you to get involved. It's really not that big a deal. They won't be coming around anymore." Casper nodded his head as if he knew this for a fact.

"If you say so, Casper." Maggie didn't like it, but she let the incident go. "Why don't you break down some of those boxes. That will keep you back here and out of Joshua's line of vision. At least it will give you some time to think up a story as to why you've got… that." She pointed at his cheek. The ice had brought the swelling down a little, but the bump was still angry and red and looked like it smarted.

Maggie kept an eye on Casper. She sent him to the post office for boxes and labels that she didn't need and to the hardware store for some varnish for the wooden bookcase that Joshua had finished. Then when he came back, she offered to buy him lunch.

"You've got to be hungry," she said. "I've had you running all over town."

Casper, looking down like he needed to conceal the bump under his eye from her, let his hair fall over his eyes.

"You don't have to," he said in such a way that it almost broke Maggie's heart.

"I've never heard of a boy your age turning down food. Here." She went to her purse that was behind the counter and pulled out a twenty from her pocketbook. "Get whatever you want from Cosmic Burger and bring me the change."

"Really?" he mumbled.

"Sure," Maggie said. She slipped her wallet

back in her purse and tucked it underneath the counter again.

"Thanks, Maggie." He flipped his hair, and Maggie was sure she saw a little smile.

"Don't mention it," she said without any expression on her face. The last thing she wanted was to make Casper feel any more self-conscious than he probably already did. With a good feeling in her heart, she watched him walk out the door and in the direction of Cosmic Burger. But when he got back, she realized that buying him lunch was not going to solve the problem he was having.

After about twenty minutes, he yanked the door to the shop open, stepped inside, dropped Maggie's change on the table, and hurried to the back of the store. Before she could ask him what the matter was, the two boys she'd seen the previous day walked in.

"This is a bookstore," the wide-set-eyed one blathered to the bulldog boy as if he were making some kind of startling revelation.

"I like books. Especially when they describe people doing it," the bulldog boy tittered. Just then he looked Maggie up and down, licked his lips, and smiled at her. She pushed her glasses up on her nose.

"Hiya. Where's Casper?" the bug-eyed boy asked.

"Casper is not allowed to have visitors during work hours," Maggie lied. There was no rule loved ones or friends couldn't stop in at any time. Heck, *she* knew half the neighborhood. Just because she wouldn't call them friends didn't mean they couldn't come in and chat with her for a minute. However, these guys didn't come across as friends. Even if she hadn't seen what they did yesterday, she knew they were up to no good.

"You see, he owes us something. He's holding on to something that doesn't really belong to him. We just want it back into the hands of the rightful owner," the bulldog said.

"What is it that he owes you?" Maggie asked.

The bulldog leaned on the counter and stared at Maggie, who narrowed her eyes at him. The fact that he was trying to intimidate her almost made her chuckle. Not because she wasn't a little nervous, but because she was so much smaller than him. Did he really think scaring her was some kind of great accomplishment?

"I don't really think it's any of your business," he hissed, and his breath smelled like cigarettes.

"If you aren't here to buy a book, then I think you should leave," Maggie said.

"Maybe I am here to buy a book," Bug-eyed replied as he walked farther into the store, looking down the aisles for Casper.

"What are you looking for, and I'll help you find it. That way you can be on your way. Let me guess, ancient Greek architecture? Maybe a complete work of Shakespeare's sonnets? Artillery of World War I? Maybe you are looking for something a little more personal… say *The Carnivorous Lamb*?" Maggie peered over her glasses at the bug-eyed boy then to the bulldog and back again.

"What's that about?" Bug-eyed asked, distracted for a moment.

"An incestuous relationship between two brothers. I believe there is a copy somewhere along the back wall by the emergency door. You look like you were headed in that way," Maggie said before pouting her lips as she pointed to the back of the store where Casper had disappeared.

"You think you're funny, don't you," Bug-eyed said.

"What's going on?" Joshua appeared in the door of the café, his hands on his hips, looking tough, sweaty, and annoyed.

"These boys were just leaving. We don't carry the books they were looking for," Maggie said quickly. The last thing she wanted was for them to start talking about Casper and giving Joshua a tip that there was a problem with their new hire.

The two young men looked at each other, then Joshua, and then Maggie before Bug-eyed walked back toward his friend and tapped him on the arm.

"Let's get out of here," he said. Bulldog looked Maggie up and down, clicked his tongue before licking his lips, and turned, following the bug-eyed boy out of the store with a hard yank of the door. The chimes jingled madly.

"What was that about?" Joshua asked as he walked toward the counter and looked out the glass to see what direction the boys had gone.

"Who knows. There are a lot of out-of-towners around for the football game. They are probably from the rival team. Family of the nickelback or something," Maggie said matter-of-factly.

Joshua leaned a little closer to her. "You mean the quarterback?"

"Whatever." Maggie shrugged. "You knew what I was talking about."

"Yeah. You're probably right. Still, this is a

bookstore. It's hardly the kind of place anyone would think to start trouble," Joshua said.

"Young people don't think," Maggie said and grabbed the stack of mail that had come the previous day that she hadn't sorted through. Joshua chuckled, nodded, and then went back into the café, talking about something that Maggie was barely listening to. She wanted him to hurry up and leave so she could check on Casper. But before she could make her way to the back of the store, real customers came in. Of course, they were chattering about the upcoming football game. Then more people came in, and before Maggie realized it, she was getting ready to lock the door for the evening.

"Good night, Maggie. Thanks for lunch," Casper said with his head down and his hair falling over his face.

"Don't mention it, Casper," she replied as she watched him snap the lock and yank the door open before she could say anything else. She hoped he wasn't leaving for good. Although she was reluctant to tell Joshua, she had come to rely on Casper, and he really did make her job a lot easier.

But the following day when she was on her way to work, she had to question who was working alongside her.

Chapter 5

It was a beautiful sunny morning as Maggie had to walk the three blocks to work. Everywhere she usually parked was still blocked off and would be for the next several days. It set her off into a bad mood. And as if that wasn't bad enough, Maggie was forced to cut through the park due to construction being done on the sidewalk. Yellow tape, jackhammers, chewed-up sections of concrete, and loud men in yellow hard hats peppered her usual path to work. It wasn't like the park was ugly or scary. It was a pretty patch of greenery with benches and flowers. The mighty oaks provided just enough shade to give a person a cool respite on hot days but enough sun to warm them up on a crisp morning like this one. Everything was very lovely, except for the dew that coated the grass.

Maggie hated the feeling of the wet blades of grass slapping across her bare ankles and, worse yet, saturating her canvas Mary Jane–style shoes that she bought at a secondhand store.

"Ugh," she said, wrinkling her face as she stepped onto the grass. On her highest tiptoes, she tried to hurry across the grass, hoping that might somehow keep her shoes dryer. It wasn't working. But just as she was about to get to the sidewalk that finally led to the street the bookstore was on, something caught her eye.

"Oh, great," she muttered. "I knew it was only a matter of time before the park attracted an unsavory element."

Up ahead of her, across the sidewalk, was a man lying on the ground. He wore blue jeans, and one clunky boot was off his right foot. His head was turned, facing Maggie as she approached, and his eyes were open. With every step, Maggie waited for the man to start blubbering something obscene or incoherent, but then something tickled at the side of her brain that she'd been trying to ignore. She knew the man. More like, she knew the boy. It was the bug-eyed boy from the day before. The adrenaline kicked in as she was sure he recognized her. The way he was staring made her skin crawl, and just as she was about to take off running back the way she came, the thing tickling her brain came into focus. There was a huge pool of rust-colored paint around his head. That same paint trickled down his neck and over his hoodie, and his white hat that was on the ground looked dark and dirty.

Maggie stopped. Before the word even formed in her mind, she started to scream. It wasn't paint at all. It was blood. The bug-eyed young man from the previous day had a huge slit across his throat with giant puncture wounds on his torso and was now dead in the middle of the park.

Within seconds, the construction workers who had been working on the sidewalk heard Maggie scream and came running.

"Are you all right, miss?"

"Holy moly, would you look at that."

"Oh jeez. Call the cops. Mike, call the cops."

"Is he dead?"

"Of course he's dead, Jake. Look at him."

Half a dozen guys in hard hats stood with Maggie. It didn't take long for the police to show up, and a familiar face emerged from the crowd.

"Gary, thank goodness," Maggie said as she

walked up to the man in uniform. Gary Brookes was one of Fair Haven's finest and had also gone to high school with Maggie.

"What the heck, Maggie?"

"I was walking to work on account that all the roads are blocked for the football game. I was cutting through the park when I found..." She jerked her head toward the body. The coroner and an ambulance showed up. One guy with the yellow letters EMT emblazoned on his black windbreaker jumped out of the red-and-white van and hurried to the body. As soon as he got down on one knee and felt the neck and then wrist of the man prostrate on the ground, it was obvious any attempts at resuscitation would be fruitless. The young man was dead.

"Go on to the bookstore, Mags. I'll catch up with you there in a few minutes. I just want to check with this construction crew to see if anyone saw anything and the crime scene stays as clean as possible," Gary said. Maggie felt a little better knowing her friend was there and that she didn't have to stay there with bug-eyed boy's bug eyes staring at her. It was almost like he was insinuating that they both knew who had done this to him.

Still in a daze, Maggie headed to the bookstore.

Normally, she liked to slip in without being noticed so she'd have a few seconds to check her hair and make sure her outfit looked nice for when she inevitably ran into Joshua. But this time, she didn't care how she looked. She yanked the door to the café open and skirted past the short line of customers to go to the back of the shop.

"Good morning, Maggie. Maggie, honey, are you all right?" Babs asked.

"Is Joshua back there?" Maggie asked as she pointed to the back room.

"He sure is, honey," Babs replied.

Maggie nodded her head and went into the back room, where Joshua was standing at the same spot where he'd planned to put the oven. There were some exposed wires in the wall and some sawdust on the floor.

"Hey, Maggie. Can you help me with… Maggie? What's the matter?" Joshua quickly rushed up to her and put his hand on her shoulder.

"What makes you think there is something wrong?" She chuckled.

"You're as white as a sheet for one. You're also shaking. Here." Joshua grabbed a stool that had been against the wall and placed it next to her. Then he gently helped ease her on it.

"There was a body in the park," she said. "You know if they didn't block off the streets so far ahead of the football game, I wouldn't have had to walk through the park. I got my shoes all wet, and my ankles are cold, and I would have never seen him. Someone else would have found him."

"Found who?"

Maggie looked at Joshua and swallowed hard. "Remember those two guys that came in here yesterday talking like tough guys and acting stupid?"

Joshua nodded his head.

"Well, someone decided they'd had enough of the one with the white hat."

"The kid with the bugged eyes?" Joshua gasped.

Maggie nodded her head.

"What do you mean someone had enough?" Joshua walked over to the mini fridge, which was in the far corner of the back room next to a table for two and a workbench. He reached in and pulled out a bottle of water for Maggie. She twisted off the top and took a sip.

"He was dead," she said and took another sip.

"Okay. Maybe he had an allergic reaction to something he ate, or maybe he had a bad heart or was diabetic and had some kind of fit," Joshua offered, his eyebrows up like even he didn't believe what he was saying.

"He was in a pool of his own blood. It was gross." Maggie frowned as she nodded her head.

"And you found the body? Oh, Mags, no wonder you are so pale. Jeez, that's no thing for a girl like you to go through." Joshua took her free hand and squeezed it. He leaned in closer to her and tucked a strand of hair behind her ear.

Just then Gary came in the back room looking for her. He cleared his throat as he approached them. Joshua let go of Maggie's hand, stood up, and took a couple steps away from Maggie as if he'd been caught cheating on a test.

"Hey, Joshua," Gary said, forcing a smile as he came closer.

"Hi, Gary. I hear you've got quite a scene out there. I wondered what all the sirens were for. Now I know." He looked at Maggie and put his arm out, palm up as if he were showcasing a new washer and dryer.

"Yeah, it's a mess," Gary replied. "Maggie, can we talk?"

"Of course. Let's go to the bookshop. I'll feel better there," Maggie said. What she really wanted was to have Mr. Whitfield back. He'd have known exactly what to do, what to say. He had been her foundation for so long that at a time like this, when the world seemed a little scarier than normal, she really noticed he was gone. Since she couldn't have him back, she could at least be surrounded by the things that he collected and cared for.

"So, tell me what happened," Gary said as Maggie eased herself into Mr. Whitfield's old chair at his desk. Gary dropped to one knee, his pocket notebook in one hand and a pencil in the other.

Maggie took a deep breath and told the story again. She tried to remember each step, each detail, every thought that ran through her head as she came upon the young man's body. A shiver raced down her spine.

"And then you said to come here. So I did," she finished.

Before Gary could ask another question, there was a loud rapping on the storefront door. Maggie peeked over Gary's shoulder and saw Casper standing there, his hands cupped over his eyebrows as he peered into the store.

Maggie pushed herself up from the chair. She walked over and snapped the dead bolt back with a loud click and yanked the door open.

"Morning," Casper said. The swelling on his

cheek had gone down significantly enough that only Maggie could still see it. Anyone else might just think he had a patch of redness due to acne or maybe even a birthmark.

"Good morning, Casper," she replied.

There was a sinking feeling in her stomach as Casper came in. He walked right past Gary to the back room where he'd fill out his time sheet. He didn't seem shocked or even curious that a police officer was in the store with his pen and paper out. Maggie looked at Gary, who also didn't seem to notice anything strange about the young man except that he was an unfamiliar face. He pointed his pen at Casper and mouthed the words "*Who is that?*" after Casper passed him.

"New stock boy," she mouthed back, wondering why Gary didn't think to question him.

That's because he doesn't know Casper knew the deceased. The words hissed in Maggie's mind. *Casper knew the dead man well enough and practically confessed to you that he was going to do something to that bug-eyed so-and-so.*

"Gary, do you know the guy's name?" Maggie asked, jerking her head in the direction of the park and the crime scene.

"His ID said Harold Beebe," Gary replied.

"Is he from around here?" Maggie asked as she pushed her glasses up on her nose.

"Unfortunately, he is a local boy." Gary clicked his tongue.

"Really? I don't think I've ever seen him around." Maggie frowned.

"He'd have no reason to come into a bookstore, Mags," Gary said and rubbed the back of his neck like he felt a headache coming on. Maggie watched him as he took a deep breath and stared at the notes he'd just scribbled down.

"What's the matter?"

After clearing his throat, Gary looked around to make sure no one was within hearing distance, scooted closer to Maggie, and tapped his notebook.

"This kid was on the sheriff's *list*, if you know what I mean," he whispered.

"I don't know what you mean," Maggie whispered back.

"Just a couple months ago, the sheriff came home to find his niece parked in a car in his driveway with Mr. Beebe. Let's just say the forbidden fruit tastes the sweetest."

Maggie was surprised. Sheriff Lee Smith was a huge barrel-chested guy who had in his younger days won several World Strongman Competitions.

Even if he hadn't been a strongman, Sheriff Smith was a mountain of a man with a bald head, thick mustache, and an attitude to go along with it. To law-abiding citizens, he was a cream puff. But to those individuals of Fair Haven who walked on the wrong side of the law, Sheriff Smith was a devastating force of nature.

"Oh my. What happened?" Maggie continued to whisper.

"Just what you'd think. Words were exchanged. Chests were thumped. Threats. And since it isn't a crime to date the sheriff's niece, there was no doubt Harold was just going to continue to thumb his nose at the man," Gary said. "The sheriff's wife was the only one who could calm Lee down. I don't know how, but she can tame that bull with a look. But I know it had Lee fuming for days that Harold was courting her."

"And now he's dead."

Gary looked into Maggie's eyes and knew they were both thinking the same thing. Would the sheriff have crossed that line onto the wrong side of the law himself to protect his family? Maggie didn't know, but the fact that Gary had the same idea meant it wasn't an impossibility.

"Yeah. But the sheriff wasn't the only person

Harold had trouble with. I can't even count how many of his neighbors and shopkeepers and fellow officers had a run-in with the boy. I don't think there will be too many tears shed once this hits the papers." Gary huffed.

Maggie wasn't sure if she should say anything about Casper's run-in with Harold Beebe. Also, where was his sidekick? Maybe he had something to do with it.

"Did he have any friends?" Maggie asked innocently. "Maybe they'll know something that can help."

Gary didn't see that she was fishing for information, or if he did, he didn't seem to mind.

"He's usually with Maynard Ramsey, who goes by the nickname Mister." Gary shrugged when he said that. Then he rattled off a couple names of people who had been seen with Harold, but from the sound of it, Maggie hadn't heard of any of them or their families.

"Maynard Ramsey. His initials are M. R., Mister," Maggie said after a few seconds of thought. Gary smiled and pointed his finger at her with a wink. "Maynard wasn't around?" she continued.

"No. At the moment, he's our number one

person of interest. But if he had anything to do with Harold's death, he's probably miles from here by now." Gary cleared his throat. "But we'll track him down. He can't run forever."

"No. He can't," Maggie said just as Casper emerged from the back room.

"Joshua left a note on my time sheet that he needed me this morning," Casper said and raised his hand to brush his hair away. Maggie saw there were bandages on his pinky and that side of his palm. She didn't say anything but instead just nodded.

It was just a few minutes before she wrapped things up with Gary, who was just about to leave the bookstore when he looked at the display window.

"Are you going to the game?" Gary asked.

"Gary, I wouldn't know what to do there even if I did want to go." Maggie wrinkled her nose after pushing her glasses up.

"You'd have a good time," he replied.

"That's what people keep saying." She shrugged.

"Well, maybe you'll change your mind. The window looks fantastic. You really are good at that... stuff." Gary smiled before giving her a nod and leaving out the door, sending the bells over the door into a happy jingle.

The compliment made Maggie smile. She'd never felt weird or awkward around Gary even through those most awkward years that were high school, where they became good friends. But no matter how good a friend he was, she wasn't about to tell him Casper knew the victim of this horrific crime. She couldn't say the newest employee at The Bookish Café and Bookstore was a killer, but she wasn't sure she could rule it out either.

Chapter 6

All day Maggie had tried to push the image of the dead Harold Beebe out of her head, but it kept resurfacing as each title she rearranged on the shelves brought it into focus. *The Headless Horseman and Other Ghoulish Tales. Slashed Promises. A Slit Between the Stars. Maigret and the Headless Corpse.* It was making her nauseous. When it was finally quitting time, her head was spinning. Casper had avoided her almost all day. She hadn't gotten a chance to ask him what had happened to his hand or even how he was feeling after the previous day.

"He's too nice," Maggie muttered as she locked the bookshop door and headed in the direction of her car, going half a block out of her way to avoid the literal scene of the crime. She didn't want to think that the guy she and Joshua agreed to hire as their stock boy and gopher could possibly be a killer. What kind of judge of character would that make her?

He had every reason to do it, her conscience echoed as if that made the pill a little sweeter to swallow.

"But a stabbing and throat slitting? That's a rage killing for sure. Could that young man actually do something like that?" Only she heard her own voice as she muttered down the sidewalk before climbing into her car. On the way home, she remembered what Gary had said about the sheriff. Sheriff Lee Smith was a nice man. But if anyone had the strength and reason to mess Harold up, he did.

"Mags, you can't just go walk up to the sheriff and say, hey, did you kill that lowlife Harold Beebe for dating your niece?" she said once she was home, walking the winding sidewalk to her home behind Mrs. Peacock's mansion.

Mrs. Vivian Peacock rented the small guesthouse behind her home to Maggie. It was a quaint little one-bedroom house with a small kitchen and living room. Just as she was about to unlock her front door, she heard the sliding of Mrs. Peacock's back door.

"Yoo-hoo!" Mrs. Peacock called. Maggie turned around and waved. Then she had an idea and started to walk toward her landlady, who was the eyes and ears of Fair View.

"Hi, Mrs. Peacock," Maggie chirped. "Did you hear the news today?" Maggie knew the Widow Peacock already had. She could tell by the look of worry on Mrs. Peacock's face and the way she was wringing her hands.

"I did. That poor boy. Nearly decapitated I heard," Mrs. Peacock said as she tugged her angora sweater tighter around her.

"Did you know him?" Maggie screwed up her face.

"My late husband had done business with his father before that man up and ran off with some cocktail waitress from Little Al's Place. You know that trashy bar down by the railroad tracks?"

Maggie nodded. She knew the bar and its reputation for being a rather tough place.

"Well, I heard the son just took up the space at the bar left by his father and fell in with a rough crowd. The sheriff had tried to steer him straight after his first two arrests for public intoxication when he was a teenager." It was like someone had put a quarter in Mrs. Peacock, and she was going to keep talking until time was up or another quarter was put in.

"Sometimes I wonder if Sheriff Smith isn't too good for his job. Just as I've always said, no good deed goes unpunished. For all his efforts, Harold Beebe didn't stop drinking but instead became even more rebellious. Until…"

"Until what?" Maggie didn't realize she was leaning forward, hanging on to every word.

"Well." Mrs. Peacock looked behind her before taking a step closer to Maggie, as if there might have been someone skulking around the corner, listening to their conversation and ready to dash back to the sheriff to report what they'd heard. "Harold kept getting into trouble, and he was just on the cusp of doing some serious time if he didn't straighten up. He was going to have a one-way ticket to *the big house*, I heard."

Maggie wanted to laugh at Mrs. Peacock trying to be hip using cop lingo. It was like putting a spiked butch collar on a chihuahua. But she bit her tongue for fear the woman may stop talking altogether.

"Sheriff Smith had tried, but the last straw was

when he came home early from work and found Harold in his house with his niece who had come to visit for a couple of weeks," Mrs. Peacock said and looked over her shoulder again. "From what I heard, Harold Beebe was in Sheriff Smith's bedroom, if you catch my meaning."

Maggie gasped. This was a lot different from the story Gary had told her about catching the young man in his car in the sheriff's driveway.

"Now, what I heard and what actually happened may be two different things. But I've never known Gloria to tell a lie. Not ever." Mrs. Peacock pinched her lips together and folded her arms over her bosom.

Gloria was Sheriff Smith's girl Friday. She handled the sheriff's office with an iron fist in a velvet glove. She'd worked and lived in Fair Haven for as long as Maggie could remember. It was almost like the sheriff's office was built around her. The small police department was in her blood and under her skin, and Sheriff Smith would be lost without her. Gloria was an attractive older lady in her sixties with salt-and-pepper hair that was complemented by the silver revolver she wore continually on her hip. And Mrs. Peacock was right. Gloria was never one to lie.

"What did the sheriff do when he *saw* him?" Maggie asked just barely over a whisper as if the imaginary person Mrs. Peacock had been looking over her shoulder for might still be there listening.

"What any normal man would do. Pulled his weapon and threatened to shoot the man. But the sheriff's niece was over eighteen. It didn't matter what she'd done or with who. She was of legal age," Mrs. Peacock continued.

Maggie felt a shiver of disgust rush over her. This sleazy young man had been in her bookstore, touching the books and the counter. She knew it wasn't right to speak ill of the dead. But if Harold conducted himself in this manner just to poke the bear that was the town sheriff, he would have stopped at nothing to get what he wanted. She might have been in more danger than she knew the day he showed his face at The Bookish Café. And what he'd done to Casper was probably just the tip of the iceberg. Maybe Casper had no choice but to stab Harold Beebe multiple times and then slit his throat. She shivered again.

"My gosh," Maggie replied.

"Of course, that is the rumor. But you certainly didn't hear it from me," Mrs. Peacock said. "Now, the real reason I wanted to talk to you. It's that time of year again when I have to pay my property taxes. I just wanted to make sure there will be no problems with paying your rent on time." She looked up from beneath her drawn-on eyebrows at Maggie.

"No. Of course not," Maggie replied as she squinted at her landlady.

"Good, because I'm on a fixed income. I don't dare pay this late, or the fees will just kill me. I'll never recover," Mrs. Peacock said before turning on her heels and heading back up to the house, wishing Maggie a pleasant evening as if she hadn't just spoken about a possible motive for the sheriff to have killed a local troublemaker.

Once inside her home, Maggie locked the door, kicked off her shoes, and went to the kitchen. Within a few minutes she had a singing teakettle on the stove. A hot cup of peppermint tea accompanied her to her bedroom, where she changed into her flannel pajamas and grabbed the book she had been rereading for the hundredth time, *House of the Seven Gables* by Hawthorne. But as she read the words that she'd nearly memorized, her mind kept drifting to the situation that had developed today.

She wondered if Sheriff Smith was distracted by the death of Harold Beebe or if he was just going about his business as if there was nothing to worry about. Who was going to continue the investigation? Was Gary digging into it? The thought made her worry for him.

"You don't even know if the sheriff did anything, Mags." She huffed after gulping down the last of her tea. Sleep finally came, but it was sporadic throughout the night. She'd catch it for fifteen minutes or maybe half an hour before it would escape her again, and her eyes would pop open. By the time her alarm went off, she felt like she'd had only two hours of sleep the whole night. But it didn't take long for her to snap to attention once she arrived at work.

Chapter 7

"Mags, honey, how are you feeling today?" Babs asked as soon as Maggie arrived at work. "I sure hope this morning was a lot quieter than yesterday."

"Morning, Babs," Maggie said with a wide yawn.

"Would you like some coffee?"

"Yes, thank you, Babs," Maggie said and shook her head to try to get some of the cobwebs out of it. She tugged at the cuffs of her sweater and wrinkled her nose.

"Coming right up. While I've got you, Mags, can I ask you a question?"

"Sure?" Maggie suddenly felt her chest tighten. She didn't know Babs that well, and although she enjoyed her big personality, Maggie never liked sentences that started with *can I ask you a question* because they were usually followed by *promise you won't get mad*. If a person had to add that phrase, maybe they shouldn't be asking the question that might make a person mad.

"I'm terrible at interior design. I'm really good at building shelves or putting in tile, but I'm just no good at the things girls should be good at. Your display window looks so beautiful, and then I look at the café…" Babs pointed to the window that had a small ledge. At the moment, there was a football on it and a football player bobblehead as the decorations.

"Did you do that?" Maggie asked, trying not to laugh.

"I did. I thought we should have something, but I'm afraid they'll egg our storefront, it's so pitiful." Babs shook her head.

The corners of Maggie's lips started to curl up as she tried not to laugh at Babs's attempt at window dressing.

"Maybe we can paint something on the window that…" Maggie couldn't hold it in and began to giggle. Just then, Joshua emerged from the back room.

"What's so funny?" he asked.

Maggie couldn't say and just pointed to the window.

"I told you that display wasn't good enough," Babs said.

"What are you talking about? You think it needs a couple more bobbleheads? Because I have a few more. Almost the entire 1985 Bears team," Joshua bragged.

"What are those?" Maggie asked.

"They won the Super Bowl," Joshua said, feigning offense.

"That's with all the commercials that are supposed to be good, right?" Maggie asked.

"Yeah, the Super Bowl is a bunch of commercials with a football game in between. That's it. I'm making it mandatory for all of my employees to attend the Fair Haven football game on Friday night."

Maggie not only stopped giggling but stopped smiling altogether. "What? That's going to be crowded, and I don't have a ticket or any money to spare. Mrs. Peacock needs her rent early because she's on a fixed income, and property taxes are due. I can't go," Maggie blabbered.

"I've decided everyone at The Bookish Café and

Bookstore is going to attend. Families are included." Joshua looked at Babs, who smiled wide and nodded her head. "Trust me, Mags. You are going to have a great time."

"Or else I'll lose my job," she muttered.

"Mags, can you help me with the window?" Babs asked again. Her eyes bounced back and forth between Maggie and Joshua, and Maggie didn't like the way her right eyebrow arched as she observed them like they were creating some kind of spectacle.

"Sure. Give me a little time and I'll think of something." Maggie smiled crookedly at Babs then looked at Joshua. He smirked at her discomfort, which made her even more annoyed. With her chin held high, she turned and went to the bookstore, snapped the dead bolt on the door open, and turned to go to her desk and confirm the inventory she'd stocked over the past couple of days.

After a few minutes, she was engrossed in checking and double-checking the titles, quantities, and ISBN numbers when the door flew open and a red-faced, stern-looking Sheriff Lee Smith stepped into the shop. Maggie's heart was stuck in her throat. She was sure Mrs. Peacock told him she was asking questions about his dealings with Harold Beebe. She was sure of it. As he approached, she felt like an ant being eclipsed by a very large, hungry bombardier beetle.

"Maggie. How are you," he said without any expression on his face.

"Hi, Sheriff," she replied and looked down after pushing her glasses up on her nose.

"I need to talk to you." He cleared his throat and strolled up to her. Maggie had never heard of the man getting violent or rough or threatening to any woman in Fair Haven. But how many women went snooping around thinking he was a suspect in a murder?

"Yes, sir?" She swallowed hard.

Suddenly Sheriff Smith stopped.

"Why, Maggie, you're shaking like a leaf. Calm down, girl. I just need to talk to that new fellow you've got working for you. He hasn't done anything to frighten you, has he?" Sheriff Smith asked.

When Maggie looked up into his eyes, she saw nothing but concern there. She let out her breath that she hadn't even realized she was holding.

"Oh no. He's a good kid," Maggie replied. Now it was time for her to clear her throat. "Has he done something?"

Sheriff Smith put his hands together like he was

giving a presentation to a bunch of schoolkids who were already impressed and amazed at the sheer size of the man and the gun on his hip.

"I'm not sure. I've got people who place him with that young man you stumbled across in the park," he said.

"Who? Who said they saw him?" Maggie blurted out the words as if she was a lawyer objecting to the opposition's line of questioning.

"Well, I'm not at liberty to say. All I know is that over the past few weeks, I've heard they'd been together. And believe me, wherever Harold Beebe was, there was sure to be trouble. Of that I guarantee," he said as he looked around the shop, as if Maggie might have tucked the boy in between some shelves or even the books themselves.

"I haven't seen him come in. He should be here any minute if you'd like to wait," Maggie replied. She watched how he looked around and tried to see if there was some element of guilt or maybe something in his eyes or voice that would tell her he was the one who did in Harold Beebe. His motive was a lot more likely than Casper getting a shiner.

"I think I'll do just that. If you don't mind, I'm going to go see Mr. Whitfield in the café." He looked again at the books. "I've got so many books at home that I haven't read yet I don't dare stay here and risk buying more."

"Sure." Maggie let out a deep breath as the sheriff made his way around the corner and slipped into the café.

Just then she heard a shuffling of papers behind her. When she turned around, she'd expected to see Poe, the cat, making himself comfortable on a stack of papers she'd be needing. But it was Casper nervously folding the parchment paper that came in the shipments of their books.

"Casper, the sheriff…" Maggie jerked her thumb toward the café.

"I heard him," Casper said and swallowed.

"He wants to talk to you about…"

"I know what he wants to talk to me about. Maggie, you have to help me. Tell him I'm not here. Tell him I called in sick. Please," Casper whispered as he nervously looked toward the café entrance. "Please, Maggie."

"Casper, he's not going to give up. I know Sheriff Smith. If you aren't here today, he'll just come back tomorrow and the next day and the next until he finds you. But by then he'll be really, really mad," Maggie said.

Casper looked like he was contemplating

bolting out the door. Maggie was sure his skin was getting slicker with sweat as he stood there. She jumped with surprise when he stepped around her and went to leave, but as if he'd been waiting the whole time, Sheriff Smith appeared and blocked Casper's only escape.

"Where you going so fast, son?" Sheriff Smith said and stared intently at Casper.

"Nowhere."

"I'd like to talk to you, Mr. Lahey. Would you mind coming with me down to the station?" the sheriff asked sternly. Even though he was asking politely, it was obvious that he wasn't really giving Casper a choice.

"I just started this job, Sheriff, and I…"

"Miss Maggie, you won't mind if I take this young man to the station for a couple of questions, do you?" All the while he spoke, the sheriff never took his eyes off Casper. The whole thing made Maggie upset.

"I'm not his boss," Maggie said, hoping this might buy Casper a few precious seconds for the tension in the air to dissipate.

"What's going on?" Joshua interrupted. "Sheriff? Is there a problem?"

"I'm sorry, Joshua, but I need to borrow your

employee here for a spell. I'd like to take him to the station to ask a couple of questions. I'll get him back to you before quitting time," Sheriff Smith said.

"Of course you can, Sheriff. Casper, just take your time. I'm sure everything will be all right," Joshua said with an understanding smile and nod.

Casper looked like he'd seen a ghost. But he nodded and walked out the door as the sheriff held it open for him. For a split second, Maggie was sure that Casper was going to take off like a wild stallion who spotted an open gate. But he didn't. He walked out and let the sheriff put him in the back of his squad car.

At least he didn't put him in cuffs, Maggie thought. She looked at Joshua.

"What do you think that's all about?" Joshua looked at Maggie as if this was nothing more than routine, as if the police absconding with an employee happened all the time.

"I think it might have to do with that man who I found in the park," Maggie muttered.

"What?"

Maggie looked up at Joshua and shrugged.

"You don't think Sheriff Smith thinks Casper

had something to with that?" Joshua looked at Maggie with his eyes bugging out of his head.

"I don't know. But those boys came in looking for him the other day," Maggie said. "And I saw them waiting for him a couple of days last week."

"Did you tell Gary when he came to talk to you?"

"I don't know. I think I did. I don't really remember. But you don't think Casper had anything to do with killing that boy. He doesn't look like he has a bad bone in his body," Maggie replied.

"No. But Ted Bundy was considered too handsome not to trust," Joshua replied.

"Yikes. Don't say that." Maggie squirmed as she tugged at the sleeves of her sweater. "I heard that Harold Beebe, the young man in the park, was a troublemaker." She went on to tell Joshua about the story with the sheriff and his niece.

"Wow. That's a kid with a death wish. I don't know the sheriff all that well, but just looking at the guy, I wouldn't cross him," Joshua said before letting out a deep breath. "Well, there isn't anything we can do about it now. If Casper had anything to do with it, the sheriff will find out."

"You don't really think he did, do you?" It was Maggie's turn to stare at Joshua.

"I don't know. You saw that cut on his hand," Joshua said.

"Yes. What does that have to do with anything?" she asked.

"When there is a rage killing, like was done to that boy from what I heard, the assailant often will have cuts on his own hands where his grip slipped onto the blade," Joshua said.

"You don't think that's how Casper cut his hand, do you?"

"I don't know." Joshua shrugged. "It's just a coincidence is all."

That stuck in Maggie's mind for the rest of the day. When Casper didn't return or call, she really began to wonder what kind of person had been working with her all this time. She could tell it bothered Joshua too. He kept rubbing the back of his neck as he was doing the tasks he'd gotten used to asking Casper to help with. Funny how after such a short amount of time, they'd grown to rely on the young man.

When lunchtime finally rolled around and there was still no sign of Casper coming back to the shop, Maggie decided to go on a short adventure for lunch. The police station was just a short jaunt away.

Chapter 8

The Fair Haven Police Station was as pretty as a postcard this bright afternoon. The black bars on the windows were beautifully accentuated by the colorful flowers in the flower box that were currently being tended to by Felix Porter, the florist who had a shop two doors down. He looked up as Maggie approached and gave her a wide smile and a wave.

"Afternoon, Miss Bell. Strange seeing you here," Felix said.

"Afternoon, Felix. I'm just here to, um, talk to Gloria for a minute." Maggie squinted and pushed her glasses up.

"No trouble, I hope," Felix replied.

Maggie shook her head, forced a smile, waved,

and hurried inside the station. It was as quiet as a church with the exception of some easy listening music coming from a small radio on the front desk. The smell of cinnamon and pumpkin filled the air. The tiny glowing flame of a candle on the counter was responsible for it.

"Maggie Bell? What are you doing here? I would have thought you'd have had enough of the police after Gary told me what happened to you. Finding that young man's body. Stronger than a shot of espresso," Gloria Teeble said as if people tripping across bodies in the early hours of the morning was a common occurrence in Fair Haven.

"Hi, Gloria." Maggie tugged at the cuffs of her sweater. "Sheriff Smith brought Casper Lahey down here a couple hours ago, and I was wondering if there was a problem. Casper didn't come back to work, and we sort of need him. If he hasn't been thrown in jail, of course."

Gloria looked at Maggie like she'd sprouted a third eye.

"Casper Lahey? He was turned loose about two hours ago. He and Lee had a heart-to-heart. Then Lee told him he was free to go."

Maggie looked at her nails and then focused on

Gloria before swallowing hard. "Gloria, can I ask you a question?"

"Sure, Maggie. What's on your mind?"

"Well, the man who was murdered, Harold Beebe. I heard that… that the sheriff had caught him… in his bed with his niece, and well, you know, it made the sheriff mad, rightfully so, of course, but that it was…"

"Calm down, Maggie. I can't believe that story has taken off the way it has. First of all, Harold Beebe had known Charlotte Smith in school. He was one class ahead of her. She and her family had moved to Philips, Massachusetts. She came back for the summer and ran into Harold in town. He followed her home, and Lee greeted him with his shotgun when he tried to step onto his property." Gloria rolled her eyes.

"That's it?"

"I'll promise you the one who made up that fantastic drama is now being sized for a pine overcoat. But you know how people would much rather believe that Lee has this vindictive streak like *Dirty Harry*." Gloria signed a couple of pieces of paper then tossed them into a metal box at the corner of her desk with the word "OUT" written in red on a white sticker taped to the front.

"Oh, I didn't know what to believe," Maggie stammered. "I never had a single problem with the sheriff. I didn't think this sounded like him at all."

"Of course you didn't. You are a bright, intelligent, law-abiding citizen. But then you've got those other people who aren't as interested in the boring truth and would rather indulge a flamboyant falsehood even if it did come from a no-good, thieving junkie like Harold Beebe." Gloria pinched her lips together. Maggie got the distinct feeling that Gloria was implicating Vivian Peacock. She wondered if there was some hostility between the two women.

"Who did Harold steal from?" Maggie asked.

"Who didn't he steal from? Before he got really deep into the drugs, he worked at Patrick Cusic's garage. Now, I can't think of a better mechanic in all of Fair Haven. But Patrick is not a guy to mess with," Gloria said. "It just goes to show how dumb Harold really was."

"What happened?" Maggie asked, hoping that Sheriff Lee or Gary wouldn't come into the station and put an end to her fishing expedition.

"Just about a month ago, Patrick had said as a favor to Lee that he'd hire Harold to sweep up around his shop, run errands, move cars. Easy work but honest work. Harold thought he was dealing with a patsy. You know what a patsy is?"

"I've read enough Sam Spade. Yes, I know what a patsy is." Maggie smiled.

"Well, Patrick doesn't sleep. He has no wife, no kids, nothing but that garage. I swear if you cut him open, he'd bleed Pennzoil. He was there late, just doing whatever it is he does at night in his own shop, and who comes busting in a window? Harold Beebe." Gloria smirked.

"Really?" Maggie gasped.

"Yeah. Really. Patrick swore to Lee that if he ever caught the kid, he'd kill him with his bare hands," Gloria replied with a smirk.

"Did... Sheriff Smith talk to Patrick?"

"If he hasn't yet, he'll get to it eventually," Gloria said. "But there are half a dozen other people Lee has to talk to first. He's got his work cut out for him. Plus, with all the people coming and going for the football game, we don't know who could have seen something and didn't realize they witnessed a crime."

"That many?"

"Harold Beebe got around and rubbed everyone the wrong way. It's common knowledge," Gloria replied.

"It really sounds that way," Maggie added and was about to ask for a few more bits of information when the phone rang.

"Oh, it's a busy morning. This is the first call all day." Gloria smirked.

"Thanks, Gloria." Maggie waved then tugged at the cuffs of her sleeves as Gloria answered the phone, pulling a pencil from the coffee mug on her desk to take a message for the sheriff. With her head down, Maggie quickly shuffled out of the station and back into the sunshine. Her shoes patted on the cobblestone sidewalk. Felix shouted a friendly good-bye that made Maggie instinctively hunch her shoulders and give a quick wave without really looking at him. Her mind was racing with the idea that there was another person who had a reason to get revenge on Harold Beebe.

"But just breaking into his garage didn't warrant an actual killing, did it?" Maggie asked.

There was only one way to find out. As she looked at her watch, she decided she had enough time left to pay a visit to Car Care Garage.

Chapter 9

The sound of metal clanking on concrete and a flurry of swear words came from the open garage door as Maggie approached.

"Don't put that there! Put it over there! No! Over there!" a deep, booming voice echoed through the high-ceilinged structure and bounced off the walls to practically slap Maggie in the face. She stopped at the edge of the garage and peered in. There were two cars on lifts high up in the air. Another car was a couple yards in front of her with the hood popped up and the driver's-side door open. A giant was stooped over it, wearing black pants and a black T-shirt, and all the swears were coming from there.

"Hold this! No! Hold it like this!" Something clanked to the ground again, and then there was no sound at all. Another guy who couldn't have been a day older than Casper came nervously dashing around the car from the other side to a workbench covered with tools and rags and hoses. He fumbled madly through all the clutter. How he could find anything, Maggie didn't know. It all looked like junk to her.

"No! It isn't over there! It's over on the *other* bench!" the man in black behind the hood yelled. "What are we doing here?"

When the young man, flustered and annoyed, looked to another bench equally covered in junk, he noticed Maggie standing there.

"Patrick!" he called.

"What!"

"Someone here to see you," the young man said and let out a long breath as if he'd just been saved by the bell.

The man who had been leaning over the car stood up and made Maggie feel like she was being engulfed by an eclipse.

"Can I help you?" he snapped as he slowly strutted up to Maggie. He was at least six and a half feet tall and built like Sheriff Smith with a big barrel chest and broad shoulders. His eyes drooped slightly at the sides while his eyebrows went up at the ends, making him look like a mad scientist. His hands were the size of catcher's mitts and were black with grease.

"Are you Patrick Cusic?" Maggie asked, looking up at the man and feeling like a Lilliputian to the monster Gulliver.

"I am," he growled.

"My name is Margaret Bell. I was wondering if I could ask you a couple of questions?" she asked and squinted up at him, as the sun was getting in her eyes as much as his gaze was making her nervous.

"What about?"

"About Harold Beebe," Maggie replied while pulling the cuffs of her sleeves over her fingers.

Patrick rocked back on his heels and looked over her head off into the distance for a second before he focused on her again. He reached behind him to his pocket, pulled out a rag, and began to wipe his hands on it.

"What about him?" Patrick snapped.

Maggie took a deep breath. "He was found dead yesterday."

"Yeah?" Patrick barked.

"I heard he worked for you and that he tried to rob you a-and…" Maggie stuttered.

"You heard? He didn't try to rob me. He *did* rob me. He stole about five hundred dollars' worth of equipment before I caught him breaking into my shop. I gave that twerp more than one chance. I gave him three chances to prove himself, and he fudged up every time," Patrick spat the words out as if it was all Maggie's fault Harold Beebe robbed him. And he didn't say fudged either, but Maggie had to turn on the censor in her mind as she never heard sentences woven in obscenities like Patrick's were.

"Do you know if he had any friends or…"

"I'll tell you something else. That girlfriend of his was in on all of it. She was just as much a junkie as he was," Patrick continued.

"Was Harold a junkie?"

"Let me ask you something. Do you think someone with their head on straight would try to rob a guy like me?" Patrick said, taking half a step closer to Maggie and glaring down at her. She tucked her chin in and shook her head. "Yes, he was a junkie. That's why he was stealing, so he could support his drug habit. And so was his girlfriend."

"What was her name?" Maggie was surprised

when the words just jumped from her mouth. She held her breath, waiting for Patrick to yell at her for interrupting.

"I don't know. Samantha or Susannah or something. She works at Little Al's Place. A real skank. There's no other way to describe her. Just trash, both of them. At least one of them is gone." Patrick sniffled and wiped his nose on the sleeve of his T-shirt. When he did, Maggie noticed a huge gash on the meaty part of his left hand.

"Did you ever press charges against Harold or his girlfriend?"

"No." Patrick stared at Maggie.

"How come? If you thought they were stealing from you, why didn't you call the police?" she asked and wrinkled her nose. To her, it was just an innocent question.

"Because I couldn't prove it," Patrick growled.

"But that's the job of the police. If you thought they were stealing and they were known to have drug problems, the police would have been able to find out," Maggie replied. "People like that don't steal something to sell it on Craigslist. They'd take it to a pawn shop. I think there are a couple just a few blocks from here. Did you ever go see if any of your tools were there?" Maggie asked as her brain flipped through various scenarios at breakneck speed.

"What? Look, I don't have time for this! I'm done. Do you hear me. I'm done!" Patrick shouted as he took a step back from Maggie, his hands up like he surrendered.

"Mr. Cusic, I just wonder if you know if…"

"Didn't you hear what I said? I don't have time for this! Why don't you go talk to the police! I've got a ton of work to get done, and no one around here knows what the fudge they are doing except me! Do you think I've got the time to go hunt down my stuff at every pawn shop in town? I don't. And I don't have time to be bothered by someone like you sticking your nose in everyone else's business!" Patrick continued to holler. His face became red, and his eyes bugged as sweat beaded on his forehead.

"You don't need to shout at me," Maggie snapped. Patrick Cusic was the meanest mechanic she'd ever encountered and vowed to never take her car to him. Plus, he might be a killer.

"What did you just say?" he bellowed before taking a step toward her.

Maggie hunched her shoulders as Patrick tilted his head and glared at her like she was on trial.

"That's no way to do business," she bit back.

"Go on! Get out of here. Go home, wherever that is! I've got work to do. I don't have time for this!" Patrick continued to shout as he turned and stomped back into his garage.

Maggie backed up and felt bad for the young man who had to work with him. No one should be talked to like that. If there was something wrong with Harold Beebe, there was *definitely something* wrong with this guy Patrick, and Maggie wasn't ruling him out as a major suspect in Harold's murder. Maybe Harold's girlfriend would know something about all of it.

"Little Al's Place," Maggie muttered as she walked back to the bookshop. When she got there, Joshua was waiting for her. Casper had called in and asked for the rest of the day off.

"I told him it was okay," Joshua said. "I'm sorry you'll have to handle the deliveries today by yourself."

"That's okay," Maggie replied. In the back of her mind, she wondered if Casper would show up tomorrow or if things were getting too hot around here.

Chapter 10

When Maggie arrived at the bookshop the next day, she was surprised to see Casper standing in the doorway.

"Good morning, Casper," she chirped as she tried to hide the surprise on her face.

"Morning, Maggie," he replied in the same awkward fashion he had a dozen times before. "Sorry I didn't come back yesterday. I had some things to take care of after I talked to the sheriff."

"That's okay, Casper. We'll get caught up today. There is a lot of heavy lifting, and I need that bookcase varnished so I can get the valuable books in it. Do you think you can do that today?" Maggie asked before she rattled off a couple more chores from the list in her head that she would need help with. Casper did nothing but nod his head. It was a matter of seconds after stepping foot inside the store that Casper had busied himself with staining the bookshelf.

Maggie watched him and how he maneuvered his hand to prevent the bandaged part from bumping into the side of the shelf. When it did, he winced and shook it out like it was wet.

While she was matching up the inventory to her lists, Maggie imagined half a dozen ways to ask Casper about his hand. She could pretend to hurt her own hand. Accidentally but on purpose, she could hit that part of his hand to make him wince and then ask what he'd done to have to use such a big Band-Aid. Instead, she decided on the most awkward and blatant method of gathering information.

"What did you do to your hand?" Maggie didn't just blurt the words out, but she cut through the silence like a chainsaw would a sapling tree and then stood there with her hands at her sides, staring at him.

"I... um... cut it trying to get into my car," Casper replied as he looked at the Band-Aid.

"Oh," Maggie replied, thinking he sounded unsure of his answer. That wasn't the explanation she was looking for. Of course, she wanted Casper to say that while he was stabbing Harold Beebe, his hand slipped on the knife, and he cut himself. But no such luck. She cleared her throat and pointed to the bathroom.

"There are clean Band-Aids in the bathroom if you need them. You don't want it to get infected," she said then busied herself in some papers that she'd found in a bottom drawer of Mr. Whitfield's desk. They were receipts dated back to 1991. She was sure they could be tossed immediately in the garbage, but she had to look them over first in order to look like her questioning was just a random act of curiosity.

A little time went by. Business was still booming, and almost every time Maggie started to work on Babs's window in the café, someone would come into the bookstore and need her help. The strange thing was that when Mr. Whitfield was still alive and a customer would drift into the store, Maggie would frown, sigh, and without saying a word, help them find what they were looking for or hold the door for them while they left empty-handed. But now, the traffic had increased so much that she was getting used to people chatting with her and even found herself smiling on occasion. No one was more surprised than her.

Finally, there was a lull. Maggie had a chance to look at the shelves that Casper was coating. The fumes from the varnish were strong, so she reluctantly propped the door open. Not only did it invite more people in but the occasional fly too.

"That's coming along nicely," she said as she squinted and looked the shelf up and down. "So, Casper, do you have any family?"

Casper looked at Maggie as if she just asked him if he saw a parade of dogs on their hind legs walking down the middle of the road ten minutes ago.

"I... don't. I don't really like to talk about myself that much, Maggie," Casper said before ducking his head and continuing to drag the paintbrush in his hand back and forth across the wood.

"I'm sorry. I didn't mean to pry," Maggie said and quickly turned and went back to her desk and the papers that were in need of shuffling.

Her cheeks were red with embarrassment. Why didn't she ease into the conversation? Maybe she should have said something about her own family? Of course, she didn't really have a family to speak of either, not now that Mr. Whitfield had passed, and his son was her handsome and handy and totally eligible boss. No. She couldn't ever say that. The fresh air coming in through the open front door was making her eyelids heavy. After a long stretch and a yawn, she looked at her watch and decided she wanted a cup of coffee and would get back to work on the café window. Quietly, she walked over.

"Babs? Can I get a small black coffee?"

"Sure, honey. I can't tell you how much I appreciate your help with the window. I have no idea what you are doing, but it already looks better than what *we* had on display." Babs giggled. "Joshua and I should stay away from decorating."

"I'll finish it right away," Maggie replied with a smile. It was hard not to smile at Babs. She was one of those people that was genuine. There was nothing fake about her, except maybe her blond hair. Maggie chatted with her for a few minutes, letting Babs talk about Earl and Roy.

"That man wanted a boy so bad. I really think he would have cried and asked for a refund if we had a girl. You don't know how much I enjoy being here in the café where I at least get a break from the baby talk," Babs said.

"I'm sure," Maggie replied and pushed up her glasses as she took a small hot coffee from Babs. She pulled a few dollars from the pocket in her sweater, but Babs waved it away.

"Joshua said no charge for staff. I think that will go for the sandwiches he wants to add to the menu," Babs added.

"Sandwiches?" Maggie asked as she started to slowly walk back to the bookshop.

"Yeah, we're going to have a small but wonderful menu here. That's what the oven is for." Babs nodded and put a hand on her hip.

Just then a couple of big guys came into the café. Maggie wasn't sure if they came for a look at Babs or if they came for coffee. She chuckled when Babs winked at her. As Maggie turned to go back to work in the other half of the building, she saw a familiar person slip in the open door. Slowly, she lifted her coffee to her lips and walked like she was on a tightrope. Carefully, she took a slow sip as she peeked around the corner.

Sure enough, the young man she thought looked like a bulldog who had been in the day before Harold Beebe was found dead was back in the bookstore and talking to Casper.

With her head down as she blew into her coffee,

Maggie quickly slipped across the threshold and behind the first row of books. Holding her breath, she listened and could hear the two men talking quietly. Since she knew she hadn't been seen, she crept closer, weaving up and down the aisles of books until she stood in the Civil War section and could hear their whispers even better.

"You don't know what you've done," Mister said to Casper. He sounded like he was about to cry.

"I know exactly what I've done. I told you there would be hell to pay, and I meant it," Casper snarled in a low voice Maggie had never heard before. Even if she had, she would have never thought it could come out of such a pleasant-looking face.

"You're going to make this bad for all of us. It isn't like you have clean hands. Yours are probably the dirtiest of them all. Especially now," Mister said.

"I'm telling you right now, if you don't get out of here, you'll be next," Casper hissed. Before any other words were said, Maggie saw Mister stomp out of the store. He looked scared and angry, completely different from the obnoxious twerp who had been acting tough with Harold just a matter of hours before.

It wasn't Casper who was afraid. It was him. But why should he be so scared of Casper? *Why do you think? He practically said that Casper killed Harold. What does "You don't know what you've done" mean?*

Maggie took a deep breath. This wasn't enough proof to go to Gary and say without a doubt that the skinny stock boy they just hired was the person who was responsible for killing Harold Beebe. In fact, there was just no way that she and Joshua could have been so wrong about a person's character. If this turned out to be true, she'd never be able to trust her own judgment ever again. It would be hopeless to ever try to cultivate any kind of friendship with anyone, let alone a romantic endeavor. Instantly she thought of Joshua. Why? Why did he pop into her head when she thought about a romantic relationship? He wasn't interested in her. Not when he had every woman in Fair Haven without a wedding ring on her finger, eighteen to eighty, blind, crippled, or crazy, looking to get him alone.

All it took was a shake of her head, and Maggie was done thinking about Joshua. At least that was what she told herself as she forced the idea of being romantic with him to the farthest, darkest corner of her mind for the time being. Right now, she had to concentrate on the situation at hand, and it had nothing to do with her love life. It had to do with the murder of a local man who had a shady past, to say the least. At this moment, Maggie didn't know what to say at all.

Chapter 11

Once the café and bookstore were tidied up and closed for the evening, Maggie pulled out the yellow pages.

"What are you looking for?" Joshua asked as he squeezed past her to make sure the back door of the bookstore was locked and the alarm was set.

"I need the exact address of Little Al's Place. I know it's off Hamilton Street, but I don't want to be driving aimlessly," she muttered with her lips pouted.

"What do you need to know about that for?" Joshua shouted from the back storeroom.

"I'm going there tonight," Maggie replied.

Her answer was greeted with silence until finally Joshua appeared in the doorway, shaking his head and chuckling. "It sounded like you said you were going there tonight."

"I did say that."

"What?" Joshua tilted his left ear toward her. "What in the world are you going there for?"

"Happy hour?"

"Mags, that place is rough. I mean, really rough. What in the world do you want to go there for?" Joshua scratched the side of his head.

"What? You don't think I can handle myself? I'm bad to the bone, Joshua. Bad… to… the… bone," she said as she wrote down the exact address of the bar and stuffed it in her pocket.

"Right. I'm going with you," Joshua said.

"I don't need a babysitter." Maggie huffed.

"Don't think of me as a babysitter. Think of me as your bodyguard because that is exactly what I'll be. Maggie, you don't know what kind of people go hang around that place. Why in the world would you want to go there? There are a dozen nice bars in Fair Haven. Come on. I'll take you some place nicer," Joshua offered, and for a second, Maggie was tempted to throw the whole investigation to the wind just to go out with Joshua. But the nagging concern for Casper was too much.

With a huge sigh that made her shoulders

slump, Maggie let her head fall forward but looked at Joshua from under her drooping eyebrows.

"I need to go to Little Al's Place," she mumbled, "because Patrick Cusik's garage was robbed, and he said Harold's girlfriend Samantha or Susannah was in on it and probably killed him," she said before raising her chin defiantly and arching her right eyebrow. It was one of the few times she didn't wrinkle her face or squint when she was talking to Joshua.

"Who is Patrick Cusic?"

"Come on. If you are going to tag along, I'll tell you on the way." Maggie huffed as they left the bookstore together.

It took twenty minutes to get to Little Al's Place. It was a two-flat-style building that looked like at one time it might have been a lovely Painted Lady–style house. But now, with the paints faded and chipped and the glowing Budweiser sign in the window, it looked like an old bar for a select group of people who knew hard times and preferred them since any other way of life would be like dropping them on the surface of the moon.

"That sounds like a real yarn," Joshua said as Maggie finished telling him what she learned from Patrick.

"I'll tell you what. If I wasn't such a lady, I'd go throw a brick through his window for the way he talked to me." Maggie huffed.

"You are a lady. That's all the more reason why we should really reconsider this plan of yours. Maggie, this place isn't for people like you," Joshua insisted.

"What? I'm not good enough to drink in a place like this?"

"No. You are too good to drink in a place like this. And you don't plan on having a drink, do you?" Joshua gasped, making Maggie feel like he'd just found a pack of cigarettes in her purse.

"That's what people do at a bar, Joshua. Even I know that," Maggie said as she put her car in park. "I hope you aren't going to embarrass me."

"Me embarrass you? That's a good one." Joshua chuckled.

As they climbed out, the banter continued, except Maggie was getting more and more annoyed with every word that came out of Joshua's mouth.

Music and the smell of cigarette smoke hit them long before they stepped up the three concrete steps to Little Al's Place. Maggie pulled the screen door open before pushing in the second wooden door that had a piece of plywood taped over where a small diamond-shaped glass window was supposed to be.

As soon as Maggie stepped inside, she realized that Joshua might have been right. There were four little round tables in the middle of the floor, each one covered in empty bottles. Big men and women in jeans and T-shirts that either displayed the words Harley-Davidson or some sports team stood nearby. The bar was on her right and had some large person perched on every stool. There were a handful of booths for two along the left wall. Every pair of eyes in the place were focused on the two clean-cut, unfamiliar faces. Maggie couldn't be one hundred percent sure, but she could have sworn that all the conversation stopped and even the music dipped for a few seconds at the intrusion into this group's sacred space.

"Come on." Joshua took Maggie's hand and pulled her toward a booth that was still cluttered with empty glasses and a full ashtray. They sat down and waited.

"Do you think they know we are here?" Maggie asked.

"Oh, they definitely know we're here. They are waiting to see if we'll leave. Look, I don't know if we are going to get any service if we just sit here. I'll go to the bar and get us a drink. You... don't... move," Joshua snapped.

"Fine. I'd like a Shirley Temple," Maggie snapped back.

Joshua let out a sigh as he shook his head. He squeezed through a couple of big guys, and Maggie watched him, hoping he didn't start any trouble with anyone. She quickly started to look around for a female among the bunch. There were a couple of rough-and-tumble-looking ladies, but they all looked too old to be Harold Beebe's squeeze unless he liked the cougar types. Strangely, Maggie had the feeling that Patrick would have made a comment to that effect had it been the situation. He didn't seem like the type to hold back out of discretion.

Finally, she spotted a woman nervously smoking a cigarette and shifting from one foot to the other at the corner of the bar. Even in the low lighting, Maggie could see she was about Harold's age, and she looked jittery.

Without thinking, Maggie got up from the booth, walked over to the young woman, and tapped her on the shoulder. She turned and looked at Maggie with her eyebrows pinched.

"Hi. Is your name Samantha?" Maggie asked.

"No," the woman snapped before turning her back.

"Sandra! Willie wants his beer!" the bartender shouted.

"Yeah, well, Willie can just wait!" the girl shouted back.

Sandra was her name. The grouchy mechanic didn't say her name *was* Samantha. He said it was something *like* Samantha or Savannah or... Sandra.

"Sandra, I'd like to talk to you for just a second if you get a minute. I'm at that booth over there. Thanks," Maggie said, pushing up her glasses. She forced a crooked smile that was not returned.

"What about?" Sandra snapped.

"Harold Beebe," Maggie replied. The look on Sandra's face was enough to tell Maggie she knew something about something.

While tugging at her sweater cuffs, Maggie bustled back to the booth like a kid who had been told to scram from the cool kids' table in the cafeteria at school. She sat down, folded her hands, and looked to the bar for Joshua.

Out of the corner of her eye, she saw a young man sidle up to Sandra and put his hand on her backside in a rather familiar manner. She didn't seem to mind when she looked over at Maggie and said something to him before shrugging her shoulders. The young man also looked to be Harold's age. Now they were both looking at Maggie, who screwed up her face in another awkward smile.

"You almost got me killed up there," Joshua said as he set down a beer and a pink fizzy drink with a cherry floating on the top.

"What are you talking about?"

"Ordering a Shirley Temple in a place like this? I don't know how I let you talk me into this," Joshua said then took his seat on the other side of the booth.

"I didn't talk you into it. You invited yourself," Maggie replied then nodded in Sandra's direction. "That's the woman I want to talk to."

Joshua looked over his shoulder. "She looks like she's been rode hard and put away wet." Joshua turned back to Maggie and took a sip of his beer before finding her staring at him with her nose crinkled up.

"What did you just say?"

"That's an old racing term. They'd say that about the horses that weren't tended to properly after running a race. The jockey rode them hard and then put them away without hosing off the

sweat. Get your mind out of the gutter, Margaret."
Joshua smirked, making Maggie blush.

Quickly, she looked away and focused on
Sandra. The girl needed to eat a couple of cheese-
burgers, and her hair could have used a trim along
the edges. With a little meat on her bones, she
would have been cute. But as it was, she was sunken
in. Maggie was sure the makeup she wore around
her eyes probably weighed as much as she did, and
the tattoos on her arms were bought with money
that could have been better spent on a couple of
halfway decent meals or maybe some vitamins.

Sandra picked up a tray that had two beers and
two shots on it and carried it over to the guy
Maggie assumed was Willie, who had been waiting
for his drinks. After setting his drinks down on the
table and walking away without a word, she
approached Maggie and Joshua.

"I haven't seen Harold," Sandra said, her eyes
darting back and forth between Maggie and Joshua
like she was watching a tennis game.

"Of course you haven't. He's dead," Maggie
blurted.

Sandra swallowed hard. "I thought it was just a
rumor."

"I was told that he was your boyfriend. Is that true?" Maggie asked.

"Are you a cop or something?" Sandra quickly licked her lips and looked at Joshua.

"No. We're not police." Maggie shook her head.

"Then I don't need to talk to you at all," Sandra said and put her hand on her hip. As soon as she did, the fellow who had his hands on her at the bar got up from his seat and started to walk over.

"No, you don't. But it's only a matter of time before the police do catch up with you about the robbery and theft at a certain garage owner's shop," Maggie said quickly. "He seemed to think that you had something to do with that. He also said maybe that was why you killed Harold."

Maggie was surprised at how easy the lie just tumbled out of her mouth. But it was obvious by the way Sandra swallowed that she did indeed know about Patrick's garage being broken into.

"I didn't have anything to do with that," she replied quickly.

"It was all Harold's idea?" Maggie asked.

"Yes. Who in their right mind would cross a guy that size with his reputation? But Harold said if he pulled it off, he'd be a legend because of who he was robbing." Sandra scratched her upper lip, turned in the direction of the guy who was slowly approaching, and waved him off as if Joshua and Maggie couldn't see her doing so. Like a trained seal, the guy stopped, leaned on a table, and just watched them.

"What was it about that particular guy?" Maggie asked.

"Patrick? He's a legend around town. They said that he had one guy come after him with a baseball bat from one side and another guy come at him with a knife. He ripped the bat from the one guy's hands and beat the other guy with the guy who had originally been holding the bat. He literally beat one guy with another guy." Sandra shook her head.

"Did you ever hear anything about that?" Maggie looked at Joshua.

"I'm still relatively new in town," Joshua replied.

"That isn't all. I heard that he made a guy disappear over something he did to Patrick's brother. No one ever had the details, but more than one person said he had a short fuse. The guy had a temper, that I know for a fact," Sandra added.

"So why would Harold work for a guy like that, let alone cross him?" Maggie asked.

"Are you kidding? Street credit. Harold wanted the reputation too."

"But Harold was just a junkie and a penny-ante dealer. Wasn't he?" Maggie asked, making Joshua look at her in shock.

"Hey, you didn't know him like I did. I loved Harold," Sandra said and was struggling to make tears surface in her eyes but just ended up coming across like she had a sneeze go back up her nose. Maggie had seen her with the man at the bar. This was all for show and was probably the same routine the police would get when they got around to questioning her.

"How long were you together?" Maggie asked.

"On and off for about eight months," she replied.

"Aside from Patrick, did you know of anyone else who might want to hurt Harold?" Maggie continued as she watched the guy from the bar inch his way closer and closer to them. The art of discretion was not his strong point, Maggie thought.

"No. Not that I know of," she replied quickly.

"Did he have anyone he hung out with? A partner in crime, so to speak?"

"Just Mister. But he and Harold were friends. I don't think he'd do anything. If I were to guess, look at Patrick. He's the one. He had the motive, and he's big enough to get it done," Sandra said confidently as if she'd really cracked the case.

"What about that kid Harold and Mister had roughed up a couple days ago? You know who I'm talking about?" Maggie asked.

"I don't know anything about that. If someone doesn't come and pay for their merchandise, then Harold will go to them to collect. It's how business is done," she said.

"The drug business?" Maggie asked.

"I wouldn't know anything about that," Sandra scoffed.

Maggie wasn't a professional detective, but she felt she read enough books to get a grasp of when someone was trying to put themselves in the best light possible in order to deflect suspicion to someone else.

"What's going on over here?" The man who had been groping Sandra at the bar finally made it to their booth. "Sandra, don't you have some drinks to serve?"

"Yeah, Tommy. I was getting to it," she said and smiled, cozying up to the guy who was just as wiry as she was with a number of tattoos on his arms and up his neck.

"You've got people waiting. You've spent enough time with these folks. Don't you think?" He looked at Joshua more intently than Maggie. She noticed that his left eye roamed a little to the left, making it look like he might or might not be staring at her.

"It's my fault," Maggie said, causing him to snap both eyes in her direction. "I was just chatting." She picked up her Shirley Temple and took a long sip, sucking her cheeks in as she did so.

"I think you two have chatted enough. Sandra, get back to work." Again, Tommy looked at Joshua. "I'm sorry you folks can't stay."

"What? Who says we can't stay?" Maggie piped up.

"You don't have to worry about us. We were just about to leave," Joshua said.

"Hold on a minute. I haven't finished my drink," Maggie said.

"That's not a drink," Tommy said. "This is a business, and we serve drinks here. If you aren't drinking a real drink, then you are going to have to leave." He leaned closer to Maggie's face. She could smell cigarettes on his breath. His teeth were yellow and clunky, stuck inside red puffy gums.

"Well, I was thirsty. I'm ready for a real drink. Aren't you?" Maggie looked at Joshua.

"I think it's getting late," Joshua protested.

"What are you drinking?" Tommy had a sinister grin on his face as he watched Maggie.

"Whatever you're having," Maggie replied confidently.

"Fine." Tommy turned and headed toward the bar.

"Maggie, have you lost your mind?" Joshua hissed. "Do you have any idea what you are doing? When was the last time you had a drink? Have you *ever* had a drink?"

"What are you getting so upset about? I had a glass of wine at the café opening," Maggie replied and lifted her chin proudly.

Before Joshua could say another word Tommy returned with two shot glasses full of brown liquid. He handed one to Maggie and held the other one up.

"Hold on. What is that?" Joshua glared at Tommy, who was enjoying himself.

"Relax, pal. She's a big girl," Tommy replied. "Cheers, darlin'."

He clinked his glass with hers and tossed the

drink back in one gulp. Then he looked at Maggie and bounced his eyebrows.

"Cheers," she said and did the same. As soon as the liquid hit her lips, she regretted her decision. But it was too late. From the back of her throat all the way down to her stomach, the alcohol burned until she could feel it pool in her nearly empty stomach.

"Here, have another." Tommy poured another one, and even though Maggie felt her throat burning, her pride made her accept the challenge.

"I think I just swallowed kerosine." She gasped as the second shot hit her even harder.

"Okay, that's enough," Joshua said.

Maggie slugged the rest of her Shirley Temple to soothe the burning sensation.

Tommy just laughed as Maggie started coughing.

"We're going," Joshua said, standing up. He took Maggie by the hand, leading her toward the door.

"The next time you come snooping around and asking a lot of questions, I'm not going to be so polite," Tommy hissed to Joshua. "I don't want to see either of you here again."

"I don't think you'll have to worry about that,"

Joshua replied as he guided Maggie out of Little Al's Place.

"I'm okay. I am," Maggie replied as she yanked her arm away from Joshua. "I'm totally okay. Fine. Did I say fine? I'm okay."

"Mags, that was probably Jack Daniels or Wild Turkey or some other kind of poison that your little body has never been exposed to. What were you thinking?"

"I was getting information. That's what I was doing. Do you know where we parked?" Maggie looked up and down the street before stopping and swaying. "Why is everything spinning?"

"Here. Hold on to me," Joshua said.

"Oh, it's about time you said that!" Maggie barked before being overcome with laughter. "I'll tell you what. I'll hold on to you if you hold on to me."

"You don't even know what you're saying." Joshua chuckled as he slipped his arm around Maggie's waist and practically lifted her off the ground to help her to the car.

"Joshua, don't act like you don't know," Maggie tittered.

"Where are your keys? I'll drive," he said as he

propped Maggie up against the passenger side of the car. "What don't I know?"

"You do know. You're just playing games." Maggie looked up at Joshua, He stopped and stared back at her.

"I'm not playing games with you, Mags. I wouldn't do that," he said softly and smiled as he tucked a strand of hair behind her ears.

"Sure you are." She poked him in the chest. "Well, I've got news for you. I think Patrick the mechanic thinks I'm pretty hot stuff. You should have seen the way he looked at me. Like I was a honey-basted ham." Maggie put her hands on her hips.

"I'll bet he did," Joshua replied with a genuine smile.

"That's right. And I know that the UPS guy also likes me, but he's really shy. He has me write down my number all the time on his little electric doodad but never calls." She pouted her lips and blinked lazily at Joshua before chuckling again as she pulled her keys from her pocket and handed them over.

"I'm surprised you don't have a line of guys trying to get close to you, Mags. I really am," Joshua said as he opened her car door for her.

"Yeah, me too. The truth?" She poked him in

the chest. "There's only one guy who I want to get close to me. Just one."

"Who is that?" Joshua asked, his voice soft as he stepped a little closer.

"It's a secret," she whispered.

Joshua inched closer still. "I can keep a secret."

"It's... someone you know," Maggie teased before awkwardly climbing into the passenger seat.

Joshua let out a deep breath, helped Maggie get her feet tucked safely into the car, and shut the door. He hurried over to the driver's side and climbed in, and within seconds, they were moving in the direction of Maggie's house.

"Do you know where I live?" Maggie slurred.

"Yes. You live at Mrs. Peacock's place," Joshua said.

"I don't live at her house. I live in her guesthouse. It's a house for one person. Just me. Alone. With no one else," Maggie said. "I go home every night, and I'm alone."

"Well, maybe some night I could come and visit. Would that be okay?" Joshua asked.

"That would be..." Maggie stopped and stared straight ahead.

"Mags? You okay?" Joshua asked, but no sooner

had the words come out of his mouth did Maggie put both hands on the dashboard.

"I don't feel very good," she grumbled.

"Oh jeez. Hold on, Maggie. Just a second," Joshua said as he pulled off to the side of the road. Before he could throw the car in park, Maggie had the door open and her head hanging out as the alcohol that had burned her throat going down was now doing the same thing coming up.

"Oh gosh," she grunted. "What did I do?"

"It's all right, Mags. Don't worry. I'll take care of you," Joshua said as she continued to expel the alcohol from her system.

But Maggie didn't know, and she didn't hear him over her own gurgles and groans. She thought it was going to be a long night. But it wasn't nearly as bad as the next morning when the sun hit her eyes.

Chapter 12

I t was a gray morning with no direct sunlight, yet Maggie felt that it was the brightest day in the history of the sun rising. Her head pounded. Her stomach flipped over at the thought of eating. The smell of cinnamon buns from down the street was enough to make her clutch her stomach. All she wanted was some coffee.

The café was already open and bustling. For some reason, Babs had the music turned up extra loud, and the customers were so busy shouting and yacking about the upcoming football game like all of them had lost part of their hearing.

"You poor thing." Babs chuckled from behind the counter. Everyone turned and looked at Maggie as if expecting to see her trudging in like a dog that had gotten caught in the rain. She squinted.

"Can I have…"

"Black coffee. Here you go. Joshua wanted me to make sure I had it ready for you." Babs stopped what she was doing, turned around, and grabbed an already made large cup of coffee with her name written on the side. "You want a little hair of the dog that bit you splashed in that?"

Maggie frowned as she took the coffee with one hand and put up the other as if she were lazily waving from a slow-moving parade float. "No."

"I'll let the boss know you are here." Babs continued to laugh and shake her head. "We've all been there, honey. And don't kid yourself. Some of these people are there with you right now."

The customers erupted in what Maggie thought was intentionally loud laughter. The truth was everyone just chuckled, but it was enough to reverberate through Maggie's head like a jackhammer. Without waiting for another comment from the peanut gallery, Maggie slinked into the bookstore where it was much quieter and took her seat in the shadows at Mr. Whitfield's old desk. Casper was already there and gave her a quiet "good morning."

"Would you please unlock the front door for me?" Maggie asked him.

She watched out of the corner of her eye as he did as he was told and flipped the closed sign to open. He was putting the second coat of varnish on the bookshelf. Maggie was sure the project didn't need her supervision. She closed her eyes and rested her head in the palm of her hand. But it wasn't long before Joshua came busting through the door with a big smile on his face and a bag from Cosmic Burger in his hand.

"How are you feeling?" he asked.

"Ugh," she muttered. Maggie was ashamed to admit that she couldn't remember anything past drinking something very small with that fellow named Tommy, who was Sandra's new boyfriend or something. The rest of it was a blur.

"I've got just the thing for you. A hamburger with everything on it and an order of fries. A chocolate shake to coat your stomach. You'll feel better in minutes." Joshua smirked and dangled the bag in front of her.

"What happened?" Casper asked.

"Nothing," Maggie managed to grumble loud enough for Casper to hear but not so loud that it rattled her teeth in her head.

"Maggie decided to take a run with the big dogs when she should have stayed on the porch. She got a little drunk last night," Joshua said as he took the contents out of the bag. Maggie hated him for tattling about her bad choice, but the smell of the burger and fries was the only thing that seemed to bring any calm to her jittery stomach. Without concern for her appearance, she grabbed the burger, unwrapped it, and took a big bite. Joshua was right. Not only did she almost instantly feel better, but she was sure this was the best burger she'd ever tasted in her life. Within a few minutes she'd devoured every bite, every fry, and was happily sucking down the chocolate shake.

"Better?" Joshua asked as he leaned against the wall, his arms folded across his chest.

Maggie nodded and, with a full mouth, muttered a thank-you.

"My pleasure. Seeing you all uninhibited last night was like a Sasquatch sighting. I'm not sure what I saw, but it was not normal." Joshua chuckled.

"Look, I was trying to gain the trust of somebody, and you weren't helping. You sat there with your tiny beer and watched as I took one for the team." Maggie looked at Joshua with her right eyebrow arched in judgment.

"Where did you go?" Casper asked. Maggie had almost forgotten that the whole reason for her adventure the night before was to find out about the girlfriend of the guy who had given Casper a shiner. Before that guy was found brutally murdered.

"Little Al's Place," Joshua replied, shaking his head.

"Why did you go there?" Casper asked.

Maggie couldn't be sure if he was suspicious or just curious. She looked at him wide-eyed as her brain came to a complete stop. There was no way she could tell him it was to find out if anyone else thought he was a killer. All she really found out was that there was some merchandise that he obviously didn't pay for that Harold was looking to collect on. The only thing it could be was drugs. That was what Harold was all about. Only drugs would get you to go up against a guy like Patrick or beat up a kid like Casper.

"I... uh..."

"I took her there," Joshua said and winked. "I thought she'd get a kick out of it. You know, seeing the kind of place most people only read about in books."

"Oh" was all Casper said. He looked at them both before he turned and went back to his project. Maggie suddenly felt queasy again. Did he know she was snooping around? Was he aware that she suspected he might have had something to do with Harold Beebe's death? She looked at Joshua, who shrugged.

"Thanks for covering for me," Maggie said quietly.

Joshua nodded and shrugged. "It was quite a learning experience, Mags. Really, it was," he said and looked at her in a way that made her skin break out in goose bumps.

"What do you mean?"

"Don't you remember?" Joshua asked, the smile fading from his lips.

"Oh no. What did I do?" Maggie swallowed hard. "We talked to… those people. I did the shot. We went to the car and… what did I say? Did I do something terrible? Other than throw up all over Hamilton Street, that is."

"You don't remember telling me about the UPS guy and all that other stuff?" Joshua asked.

"What? What did I say about him?" Maggie asked, getting very concerned that the food she just ate was going to come back up. What had she done last night? What had she even been talking about? Had she made an even bigger fool of herself than she imagined?

"Oh, well, it was nothing e-except you said that you thought Patrick was interested in you, and I thought if he was that I'd help you get to know him," Joshua stammered.

Maggie looked at him and frowned. She began to laugh. "You must have misunderstood. I can't imagine him liking anyone."

"Oh, I might have heard you wrong. You weren't exactly pronouncing all your words," Joshua said.

"I'm never doing that again." Maggie shook her head.

"That's good to know. Now, after all that, did you find out what you wanted to?" Joshua asked.

"I think I'm going to have to talk to Gary," Maggie said.

"And tell him what? That you are helping with the case?" Joshua asked.

"You don't need to worry about what I'm going to tell Gary. You see what happened when you invited yourself to go out with me yesterday. I could have been in and out of that place without a single incident. But you came along, and the next thing I know, I'm Dean Martin at a roast."

"How old are you? Dean Martin was way before your time," Joshua said.

"So, what does that mean?"

"It means… you really need to get out more with people your own age," Joshua said.

"What are you talking about?"

"The only time I've ever seen you go out was… well, last night. And it was just to snoop around," he whispered. "Haven't you ever thought of going out for fun? I told you everyone has to come out to the football game. I mean it. If you don't come, there will be some serious consequences." Joshua huffed.

"That is unconstitutional, you know. You are just my employer, and once I'm off the clock, my time is really my own," Maggie replied, putting her hands on her hips, even while she was still sitting at the desk.

"I'm just your employer. Is that so? Fine." Joshua clicked his tongue and shook his head. "As your employer, I'm telling you to finish with the receipts. I need them for deposit, and then I'll need your updated inventory on the new books and what we need to buy."

"We could scale back on the new books and get

some more classics in here," Maggie muttered as she avoided Joshua's eyes.

"That's fine," he replied.

"Fine," Maggie said.

"Fine, Margaret!" Joshua shouted over his shoulder as he went into the café.

Maggie cleaned up the wrappers of the food he gave her and took a last sip of the chocolate shake before the straw made that sad guggling sound that accompanied an empty cup. After throwing all the garbage away, she stood up and was grateful the room and her stomach were no longer tumbling over themselves. But in her heart, she felt a slight ping of regret. She didn't mean to snap at Joshua or tell him making her go to the football game was unconstitutional. Of course, if it meant being with Joshua, she wanted to go.

But once again, she screwed things up and made herself look like a spoiled brat. What was it about Joshua that made her get that way? Just because he was handsome and handy and made her laugh didn't mean he was the end-all, be-all of the male species. Just because he brought her a burger and fries after she'd drank too much and had a hangover like a sorority girl during pledge week didn't mean he deserved an award.

But he didn't embarrass you after you embarrassed your-self last night, her conscience needled her. She wanted to go tell him she was sorry, but her pride wouldn't let her. Instead, she needed to figure out a way to talk to Gary and get him to give her the address of Maynard Ramsey, also known as Mister.

Chapter 13

Gary looked up from his desk the minute the door to the police department opened. Gloria gave a friendly salutation.

"I'm surprised to see you here again. Two times in just a couple of days. I hope you aren't having any trouble, Maggie," Gloria said.

"No. No trouble," Maggie replied with a crooked smile. "I just wanted to talk to Gary for a minute." The officer straightened at his desk and smiled pleasantly.

"This *is* a surprise. What can I do for you Maggie?"

"I wanted to talk to you about Harold Beebe," Maggie said.

Gary set aside the papers he was working on and put his pen in the coffee mug on his desk that held a dozen other pens and read "Fair Haven's Finest" on it.

"What's on your mind?"

"Where does he live?" Maggie was sorry she blurted out the words.

"What do you need to know for?"

"I'm wondering if he lives close to…" Her mind reeled as she tried to think up a simple lie, nothing earth-shattering that would cause the angels to weep. An innocent white lie. "If he lives close to Mrs. Peacock. She is convinced the boy is going to seek retribution on me for finding the body and reporting it. There is no talking to her, but she's sure that something is going to happen at her house or the guesthouse where I live."

Gary looked at Maggie. It was a horrible lie, but it was the best Maggie could come up with. She'd tried to think of something on the walk over. Nothing would come to her, and there was no time to waste. Once she walked into the station, she had to just hope a kernel of an idea would take root. It did, and it produced a pitiful fruit.

"What? Now why would she be worrying about that?"

"Well, I don't think she's too far off, Gary. From what I've heard around town, he's not the kind of guy to mess with. Plus, he's got to be one of your main suspects, right? The main suspect in a murder. We're not just talking about some guy who stole some beer from the Fair Haven liquor store. This is serious." Maggie nodded before pushing her glasses up on her nose.

"What does Mrs. Peacock think she's going to do? Go over to his home and give him a strict talking-to about staying off her property? That ought to scare him straight," Gary snickered.

"No. Of course not. I think she just wants to know what area he's from. You know how Mrs. Peacock likes to know what's going on around town and who is doing what." Maggie shrugged.

"I can't give out that information, Mags. You know I can't. But if it makes Mrs. Peacock feel any safer, just tell her the chances are pretty good he's going to stay there until this whole case is settled." Gary patted Maggie's hand.

"Okay." Maggie sighed.

"Is there something else?"

Maggie didn't know what to say. She couldn't just come right out and ask him for Mister's personal information now that she'd told such a fib.

But maybe the truth was a better route to take. Just as she was about to open her mouth and confess, letting Gary know her real motive, two very angry men in flannel shirts came bursting in through the front door.

"Where's the sheriff?" the first man shouted at Gloria, who immediately stood up, put her hands on her hips, and glared at the men.

"Mr. Heatherford. Mr. Dominick. You do not come pounding into my station like a couple of ornery bulls let loose in a cow pasture. Now, what's the problem?" Gloria asked.

"Just a second, Mags. These two guys have been feuding over their property lines for the past two years. They're in here at least once a month," Gary said and stood up from his desk to give Gloria any necessary backup she might need. Maggie took a deep breath and didn't turn around to face the commotion. Instead, she stayed at Gary's desk, her eyes scanning over everything until they stopped on his little pad of paper that he always had with him to record his notes. It was the same one he scribbled in when he took her statement.

With a quick glance over her shoulder, she made sure no one was looking at her. Gary and Gloria had their backs to her, and the arguing neighbors were too busy pointing their fingers at one another to even notice her. Slowly she stood up, grabbed the notebook, tucked it into the sleeve of her sweater, and hurried to the bathroom that was just across from the holding cell.

Once inside with the door locked by a tiny silver latch, she pulled out the notebook and began to flip through the pages. She came across the notes of her own statement. Any conversation about Mister would have to be past that somewhere.

"My gosh, Gary. How do you even read your own chicken-scratch handwriting?" she muttered and pressed her ear to the door. Hearing the neighbors still arguing told her she had a couple more minutes to decipher this handwriting and find what she was looking for.

Every page had something different, and some notes didn't even apply to the Harold Beebe case. Just as she was about to give up and assume that Gary didn't have anything on Mister, she came across an address all by itself. It read Ricmorris Commons. #34 Ratcliff, Collidge Road.

"This has to be it. Everything else makes sense, but this is all by itself and makes no sense. Well." She shrugged. "What have I got to lose?"

Maggie had no idea how long she'd been in the

bathroom. To make it look like she was in there for the usual reason, she flushed the toilet and ran the faucet for a few seconds before she tucked the notebook back up her sleeve. It was almost silent out in the bullpen of the station. Only Gloria's voice could be heard as she commented on Mr. Heatherford and Mr. Dominic paying them a visit and threatening lawsuits over leaves falling from one tree onto the other's yard.

"I don't know where those old geezers get the energy," Gloria said.

"Neither one has ever talked about moving. I think it's this constant fighting that keeps them charged. Like they feed off each other." Gary chuckled as he approached his desk just a few steps ahead of Maggie. Immediately, he saw his notebook was missing.

"What are you looking for?" Maggie quickly asked, knowing exactly what was gone from his desk.

"My notebook," he said before leaning over his desk to rustle up a couple pieces of paper in search of the pad. Maggie stooped down on the floor like she was tying her shoes, even though they had no laces on them. With one hand down by her ankle, she quickly pulled the notebook from her cuff with the other.

"Is this it?" She reached up to him, looking into his eyes and innocently blinking as she handed it to him.

"How did it get down there?" he asked suspiciously.

"I don't know," Maggie grumbled and wrinkled her nose as she stood up. "You aren't very organized. I think we have a couple books in the self-help section about getting things in order in your life."

"Very funny, Mags." Gary smirked.

"I'm not trying to be funny."

"You should get that book, Gary," Gloria piped up without turning around from her desk.

Maggie wasn't sure if Gary knew she'd peeked at his notes. Was that a crime? Was it top-secret information, like a diary? It wasn't like Maggie tore pages out of it. She memorized the address. Plus, for all she knew, it was the address of a new girl Gary was seeing. That thought made the hairs on the back of her neck stand up and sent ripples over her heart when she thought it.

What do I care if Gary has a girl? Maggie thought. She didn't, did she? No. She didn't.

"What is this? I have a very intricate system of doing things. There is a place for everything, and everything in its place," Gary said.

"More like everything all over the place." Maggie huffed as she walked toward the door.

"That's all? You're leaving?" Gary said as he looked at Maggie.

"Yes," Maggie replied. "Bye, Gloria."

"See you later, Maggie. Take care," Gloria said as she took a file from the top of a small stack on her desk.

In a swish of air and the sound of the door shutting, Maggie was gone.

Chapter 14

Maggie knew the Ricmorris Commons. A good number of young people of Fair Haven had rented an apartment there at one time or another. The units that snaked around in the shape of a "U" that, from a bird's-eye view, made a four-leaf clover were rented by the month. Turnover was high. Occasionally, when the months were hot, the police would be called. There would be drugs or a domestic disturbance, and some arrests would be made. It wasn't a totally crime-ridden building, but there was an unsavory element that could often be found creeping along the parking lot or skulking in the doorways.

The sun was still up, but a blanket of gray clouds had stretched across the sky, giving it an ominous appearance. Maggie didn't think it would be wise to drive her car into the close-knit community, winding around the paths that wormed around with no rhyme or reason, peppered with speed bumps, only to get lost or cornered when she needed to make a break out of the place. It wasn't worth it. Instead, she parked her car in the parking lot of the feedstore that was just across the property line on the northern end of Collidge Road.

The fact that Maggie had no idea where #34 Ratcliff was inside the complex did not prevent her from getting out of her car, walking across the grass, and squeezing through the narrow gangway between the first set of buildings to begin her search.

As Maggie walked across the first courtyard, she began to feel a crazy sensation that she was being watched. The numbers on the doors didn't go in the right order. Whoever designed the Ricmorris Commons had added a strange numeric pattern that was as difficult to decipher as the World War II Windtalker codes.

Finally, after getting more than frustrated and feeling like she was walking in circles, Maggie made a bold move. The two young people sitting on folding chairs outside one open apartment unit had been there since Maggie first started looking around. She was sure they had been watching her but made no attempt to confront her. So she walked up to them as confidently as possible.

"Can you tell me where apartment number thirty-four is?" she asked.

Music came from the inside of the apartment, and the smell of cigarette smoke came not only from the dark place but from the two people sitting there. One was a young woman in jeans and a T-shirt. Her hair was wet like she'd just gotten out of the shower, and her nails were a chipped bright pink. The young man sitting on the other chair had long hair, too, but it was dry and combed neatly into a ponytail. He had a long face that appeared too big for his body.

"Thirty-four is down that way and to your left," the woman replied and pointed down the sidewalk to the neighboring bank of units. Neither one of them smiled or gave any further instructions.

"Okay, thank you," Maggie replied. "Do you know if Mister is home?" She didn't know why she asked these people about him. Part of her wanted to make it clear she wasn't just there to slum it. She was there for a purpose. A young man was dead, and Maynard Ramsey knew that young man. And what was there to be afraid of anyway? These were two kids in their late teens, early twenties at the most. Neither one looked like they could lift a cat, let alone fight.

"What do you want to see him for?" the young man asked. Suddenly, Maggie wasn't so confident about the abilities these two people might have when it came to doing harm.

"I wanted to talk to him about a personal matter," she replied and gave a crooked smile. Neither one of them smiled back, crooked or otherwise.

"Don't know if he's home or not. Don't know if he's even staying in that apartment still." The man shrugged and looked up at Maggie. His eyes were set too close together.

Maggie nodded. "Well, there is only one way to find out. Thanks for your help." Without waiting for them to say anything else, Maggie headed off in the direction they had pointed. As she walked, she could feel their eyes on her. Someone could be heard talking on the phone in one apartment as she passed by, and the television was on some silly game show in another.

Finally, Maggie found unit thirty-four. It was at the very end of the string of units in this section.

After looking around and assuming the coast was clear, she pressed her ear against the door and listened. Nothing stirred. She knocked politely on the door and waited. There was no response. This only spurred her on to knock a little louder, but still, there was no sound of movement from inside. Her recollection of Mister's behavior in the bookstore made her feel like she was entitled to show some aggression. He had, after all, barged in and made a scene acting tough and obnoxious. How would he like it now that someone had come to his place and started doing the same thing? Pounding on the door might have been excessive, but Maggie didn't care. Just as she raised her fist to start banging, movement out of the corner of her eye caught her attention. She looked and saw a police car approaching.

Had someone from inside called the police on her? Did those two numbskulls from the other unit put the call in?

"What are you saying? The chances of the cops being called on you are slim, Maggie," she muttered and quickly looked around. This was probably nothing more than a routine cruise through the area to keep the trouble to a minimum. But still, the squad car kept getting closer. Finally, Maggie decided she didn't want anyone to know she was there. Quickly, she slipped around the side of the building. It was like the gangway she had originally walked through. Her heart started pounding as she heard the car getting closer. She pressed her back against the bricks and looked around for a place to hide. There was a dumpster that had been tagged with graffiti and a couple of skids that looked like they'd been there since the building's construction. The wood was rotted and warped. The idea of climbing in the dumpster made her stomach flip. But the sound of approaching wheels was even more upsetting.

"That's going to be the first place they look." Maggie tried to convince herself there was no reason to climb in. She took two quick steps toward the metal behemoth and lifted the lid, but the smell of rotting food and heaven knew what else quickly turned her around. She couldn't do it. Better to take her chances with Fair Haven's finest than climb in that mouth of decay and stench. She'd never get that smell out of her hair. So she waited.

The police car did pull up in front of apartment number thirty-four. Maggie peeked and watched Sheriff Smith get out from behind the steering wheel. He opened the back door of the car, and Maynard Ramsey poked his head up.

"We aren't going to have more silly attempts like this last one, are we, Maynard?" Sheriff Smith hissed as Mister emerged. He looked like he'd been crying and maybe his cheek had been slapped.

"No," Mister muttered. He didn't look like the punk that had come into the bookstore. He looked like a terrified and humiliated child.

"I didn't hear you. What was that you said?"

"I said no, Sheriff," Maynard replied.

"That's better. Do you know how much easier this makes things for me? If you would have only done what I'd asked you all those years ago, you might not be in this predicament. But here you are. And now I'm holding all the cards," Sheriff Smith taunted. Maggie watched, careful not to be seen, and held her breath.

"What happens if they find out?" Maynard whimpered. Maggie was sure he was going to burst into tears any second.

"Toughen up, Maynard," Sheriff Smith said and roughly patted Maynard on the cheek. It wasn't a pleasant tap but more like a slap to get him to sober up.

"But Sheriff, I…"

"Don't but-sheriff me. You knew what you were getting into. This is called the big leagues, and you are in them. Up to your eyeballs. So pull yourself together. I don't want to make another trip out here to give you a talk. Because believe me when I tell you, there isn't going to be another chance. This is it. If you do this, there may be a chance for you to experience freedom. If not, I hope you like the color orange and crowded showers."

Maynard ran his hand over his head. He walked away from the sheriff up to his front door. He turned around to face the sheriff.

"But what if they catch me?" Maynard whined.

"Maybe you should have thought of that before you made a deal with the devil," Sheriff Smith said.

Maggie had never seen him like this before. He looked like he was enjoying talking to Maynard Ramsey this way. And from what they were saying, Maggie wasn't sure this was an honest, law-abiding situation that they were discussing. Had she been wrong all along about the sheriff? Here he was, driving around the person Maggie would have guessed was the main suspect in a murder and telling him he was going to do as the sheriff told him. It didn't look good from any angle.

"Aren't you going to do anything?"

"Maynard, you brought this on yourself. I told you you'd screw up, and I'd be there waiting. I'm giving you the best option you'll ever get. You think living in your mama's apartment is going to keep you safe for very long? Heck, I'm sure half the town knows your address by now. All you have to do is this one thing. This one little thing, and I'll make sure you get what we discussed. And maybe I won't need you for anything else."

"Isn't there another way?"

"No. It's my way or the highway. The problem for you, Maynard, is that you know, and I know you'll be dead before you even get to the off ramp. I don't tolerate a man who won't make up his mind. You can't have it both ways, Maynard. You will do what I'm telling you, or there will be a world of hurt waiting for you. I kid you not. You will be dead within twenty-four hours. There is no turning back."

There were a few mumbles that Maggie couldn't understand, not that she was really listening anymore. The fact that Sheriff Smith had threatened Maynard with death was enough to stop her brain from thinking. He had to have something to do with Harold Beebe's murder, and from the sound of it, he was tying up all the loose ends. Maggie slowly let out a deep breath as the sheriff got back in his car.

Maynard jingled some keys and went into his apartment. He shut the door behind him quietly, and after a series of locks were slipped in place, Maggie was sure she could hear him crying. What was Sheriff Smith doing that would make a punk like Maynard cry? It had to be bad. Maggie hurried back to her car. Her mind was swimming as she faced the fact that some of the people in her little town might be evil to the core. This was becoming a tangled web that she was sorry she'd gotten involved in.

"You didn't ask for this, Mags. You literally nearly tripped over it. Harold Beebe, that is," she mumbled. There was no way she could go right home. Her adrenaline was racing in her veins, and she just needed to be out with other people for a short time. The grocery store was open. It sparked her memory that she needed some milk.

Stepping inside the bright building made Maggie's nerves settle. She took a deep breath as she slowed her footsteps to help calm her nerves. As she wove her way through the aisles, she pushed aside the sound of Maynard sobbing inside that cheap and dingy apartment and the words Sheriff Smith had hissed at him and decided to make her way to the shelves of junk food.

"Something chocolate," she muttered as she looked up and down the shelves. Hostess Ding Dongs were exactly what she was looking for. But as she reached up to grab a box for herself, she felt an ominous shadow quickly approaching. When she looked to her left, she gasped.

"You! I've been looking for you!" Patrick the giant mechanic came stomping up to her, pointing his fat sausage finger right at her.

"What are you talking about?" Maggie snapped as she leaned back into shelves of cinnamon cakes and Swiss rolls.

"Isn't it funny that right after you come to my shop, someone tries to break in again? I find that more than a coincidence!" he yelled.

A few people stared at them as they pushed their carts past. Others peeked around the endcaps to see what all the noise was about.

"I don't even know you. Maybe someone tried to rob you because you are a jerk. Did you ever think of that?" Maggie replied.

He was still wearing nothing but black. A black T-shirt and black pants. His hands were still dirty with grease, and the veins were still popping on his head while his eyes bugged and his face turned red.

"I know your name, Margaret Bell. You're that

little bookworm at that bookstore," Patrick growled. "You're always snooping around in people's business. You don't know when to mind your own business, do you? Trust me, you're going to learn a lesson."

"I don't know what your issue with me is, but I didn't have anything to do with your shop getting robbed. Maybe you've got lousy security. Maybe you are a terrible judge of character, and the people you are friends with aren't really your friends. I guess that was the case, because I can't see someone like you having any real friends." Maggie huffed and crossed her arms. She stared almost straight up into Patrick's face and wondered how it must have felt to be that tall and look down on everyone.

"What did you just say?"

"And you are hard of hearing too."

Patrick leaned down to get closer to Maggie's face. She pulled her chin into her neck and frowned.

"I'm not afraid to make an example of someone who thinks they can cross me," Patrick said just over a whisper.

No one in the store came to see what the hubbub was about. It shocked her that in this town, where everyone knew almost everyone else, no one stepped in to tell Patrick to calm down and go about his business.

For a second, her heart jumped, as she was sure he was going to do something that would leave a lasting effect on Maggie if she didn't get out of there.

"Patrick! What do you think you're doing?" Casper shouted.

Patrick straightened and looked at Casper as if he was watching a unicorn with a leprechaun on its back advancing toward him. He stared with his jaw slack, and Maggie thought he looked like Neanderthal Man.

"Oh, you. Yeah, I know all about you too," Patrick barked at Casper. "You're one of the dead kid's friends."

"Seems like you are the one in everyone else's business," Maggie grumbled. It got her a glare before Patrick focused again on Casper.

"Are you all right, Maggie?"

"Yes. Colossus was just about to get out of my way," Maggie replied before she turned, grabbed her box of Hostess Ding Dongs, tucked it under her arm, and went to step around the man. But he wasn't done with her or Casper.

"You hang around him, and you're going to end

up like that guy they found in the park," Patrick grumbled with a mean grin on his face.

"What do you know about it?" Maggie asked, quick as a whip, and pointed to the fresh bandage on the fleshy part of his right hand. He looked down at her before taking a couple steps back. He looked at Casper then at Maggie again before turning on his heels and stomping away.

"Come on," Maggie said and grabbed Casper by his sleeve. They stayed far enough behind Patrick just to see him get into a gold-colored, dented SUV. As they watched him ooze into the front seat behind the wheel and slam the door shut, Maggie shook her head.

"You'd think as a mechanic he'd have a nicer-looking car," she said and looked at Casper. He didn't say anything but instead cleared his throat.

"I have to go," he replied and started walking.

"Well, at least let me give you a lift. It's getting dark, and some of the streets aren't safe. Especially with that big galoot clomping around." Maggie smiled and tucked her box of Ding Dongs under her arm to pull her keys from her pocket.

"No. I... have... a car," Casper said and kept walking.

"You do? What kind of car do you have?"

Maggie took two steps before Casper turned on her. His hair had fallen over his eye, making him flip it away with a jerk of his head.

"Maggie! I don't need you following me around. Just back off!" he said before he turned and clomped off toward the farthest part of the parking lot.

"Ma'am, can I see your receipt for those?"

Maggie heard a deep voice behind her. She turned around and looked up into the face of a flat-faced man in a neon-orange-colored vest.

Maggie walked back inside the store, wondering what had just happened and how many people were capable of murder in this town. She had yet to narrow it down to anyone. Everyone involved looked capable of killing someone. What connected them to Harold Beebe? Casper was bullied by him. Patrick was almost robbed by him. The sheriff had a personal vendetta against him. There had to be someone out there somewhere who held the key. The only person Maggie could think of was Maynard Ramsey, and she had the feeling if she approached him, he'd have nothing to say. Why would he spill his guts to a bookworm when he had the sheriff threatening him?

Chapter 15

That night, Maggie couldn't sleep. By the time the sun started to lighten the sky, she was already at the café, putting the finishing touches on the window display. She kept replaying all the scenes from yesterday. They sent her in a million directions at once. What was Sheriff Smith doing with Maynard, and what was he threatening him for? Why did Patrick make a point to come after her when he thought someone had tried to rob his shop again? And what was wrong with Casper? All she did was try to help him get home. The only person out of the whole motley crew that she felt sorry for was Maynard, and that guy was obviously too scared to be a bully anymore.

So when Gary appeared in the window, it gave her a start.

"What are you doing out so early?" she yelled through the glass.

"Open the door," Gary replied and made a fist he brought to his face to yawn into.

Maggie hurried and snapped the latch on the café door. The morning air was crisp and sent a shiver over her shoulders when she pulled the door open. Gary slipped in and yawned again.

"Why are you on duty at this hour?" she asked.

"Do you have some coffee ready?"

"No," Maggie replied, wrinkling her nose.

"Can you make some?" Gary asked with his eyebrows raised, looking pitiful.

"I don't know how to work their fancy state-of-the-art coffee maker." Maggie huffed. "But I think I can cobble something together."

"Anything to keep my eyes open," he said.

"Why are you working so early?"

"I never went home last night. I kept getting call after call. With all these tourists that have flooded the place for the football game, it's like Mardi Gras out there. I was at Little Al's Place about three times to break up a couple of shouting matches over the course of the night. Every time I thought I'd be able to call it quits, I'd get another hit over the radio. It's a madhouse out there."

Maggie bustled around at the microwave before returning with a steaming mug.

"Was there a full moon last night?" Maggie asked.

"If there was, I didn't see it. But judging by the way people were behaving last night, it might have been." He took the cup from her hands and took a sip of the brown liquid. He swallowed and grimaced. "What is this, Maggie?"

"Instant," she replied.

"How old is this stuff?"

"I don't know. I didn't look. It's freeze-dried crystals. They don't go bad," she replied and yawned herself.

Gary shook his head and reluctantly took another sip. "How come you are here so early?"

"I couldn't sleep," Maggie replied and went back into the café.

"Did Joshua come down to help you with the window?" Gary asked as he slowly walked over to see what she was doing. Maggie had painted the glass to look like a locker room with the jerseys of famous football players hanging in the lockers or across the benches. It looked great.

"No." She looked at him and smirked.

The idea of Joshua doing anything like paint or decorate made her chuckle. She'd been quiet upon entering the café, since Joshua had taken over his father Mr. Whitfield's upstairs apartment on occasion. And she put her index finger to her lips then pointed to the ceiling, letting Gary know her employer was probably upstairs sleeping.

"How about Casper? Did he help with any of this?"

"No. I'm not sure what Casper's deal is. He's good around the bookshop and the café. He'll do whatever we ask. But he's strange. Like he's got a secret."

Gary took another sip of the bad coffee and cleared his throat as he choked it down. "I had to go to Hickory Creek because someone said they saw a suspicious character throwing something off the bridge."

"My gosh. That's dangerous. Did they say what he looked like?" Maggie asked.

"Yeah, they said he looked like Casper," Gary said as he looked over the rim of his coffee cup to see Maggie's response. She looked at Gary with surprise.

"That's odd. Why would Casper be throwing

stuff off the bridge?" Maggie shrugged and looked at Gary like he'd just asked her to pick up the front of his squad car with her bare hands.

"Not stuff. Something. One thing. I was told it was a knife." Gary looked into his coffee cup and swirled the last of the liquid inside it.

"There are a lot of tall, wiry guys in Fair Haven, right? It could have been any number of young men. And how did they know it was a knife? It could have been just a stick or maybe just a piece of metal that was on the ground. Who gave you the tip?" Maggie grabbed her paintbrush and was about to continue painting, but her hand was shaking.

Tell him what happened, her conscience prodded. *Tell him how strange Casper was acting. It might be important.*

Just as Gary opened his mouth to speak, there was static over his radio.

"Yes, Gloria. I'm here," he replied as he handed his nearly empty cup to Maggie, who listened and heard Gloria rattle off a couple of numbers that meant something to Gary and nothing to her.

"Roger that. I'm on my way, and then I'm going home. Lee will have to handle the rest himself. Over," he said and shook his head.

"Copy. Over" was Gloria's reply.

"What's happening?" Maggie held the cup in both hands. She'd never seen Gary look so tired, but even without sleep, he managed a smile and a wink. His five o'clock shadow from the previous evening made him look rugged and tough. Different from the clean-shaven guy he usually presented to the world.

"Someone reported seeing a couple of people loitering in the park. Since they found Harold Beebe's body there, the local teenagers who listen to heavy metal and wear black all the time are convinced his spirit is still roaming around." Gary yawned. "So we've had to chase them out of the park, confiscate whatever tiny bit of drugs they usually have on them, and tell them not to come back after hours. What kind of morbid teenager wants to hang around a crime scene?"

"Yeah. Whatever happened to sock hops and root beer floats at the corner drugstore?" Maggie huffed and put her hands on her hips before she was gripped by a yawn that stretched her mouth wide. She blinked and looked at Gary, who was smiling.

"You don't know how cute you are, Mags," Gary said and scratched the side of his face. "I'll see you later. But before I go, what do you know about Walter Payton, Knute Rockne, and the Terry Bradshaw?"

"Nothing. They were just on the covers of some of the books Joshua bought and made me put on display." Maggie shrugged.

"Well done." He winked before he left the café with Maggie just standing there. Although she heard Gary's compliment, it didn't resonate like his comment about the people in the park trying to summon the ghost of Harold Beebe. It gave her an idea that was like a vitamin B shot. Suddenly, she was more awake than she had been all night and was eager for the next night to come.

Chapter 16

Maggie was able to go home after work and get a few hours of sleep before she headed to the place where Harold Beebe breathed his last. Both Joshua and Babs loved the window, and over half a dozen patrons who came in for coffee and a pastry commented on the displays in the café and the bookstore. It made her feel good, especially when Joshua came up to her.

"I didn't think you could make the window look almost as good as this display in the bookstore. But it is amazing," he said at the end of the day when Maggie was at the counter, sitting with Poe in a square of late-afternoon sunshine.

"Thanks," she replied and pushed her glasses up on her nose.

"I'm continually amazed by you," he said as he headed to the stairs that led to the upstairs apartment. "I can hardly wait for the next surprise you are going to spring on me."

Had it been any other night, she would have been bouncing on cloud nine after a compliment like that. But Maggie had too much on her mind. She was certain that she'd find someone skulking around the park after dark in the wee hours, visiting the scene of the crime. Why she hadn't thought of this first, she wasn't sure.

"Because you aren't morbid, Mags. That's why," she said.

She drove home, where she ate a quick bologna sandwich, took a catnap, and set her alarm for two thirty in the morning. She'd read enough books to know that although midnight was considered the witching hour, three a.m. was the Devil's hour. It had to do with Christ dying on the cross at three in the afternoon, so the flip side of that was three in the morning. Evil supernatural powers were said to be fast at work then. The thought sent a shiver over Maggie's back but did not deter her from going. She dressed in black stretch pants that she rarely wore and a long black sweatshirt she had used as a Halloween costume for several years in a row. It was black. That had been good enough. No one ever came into the bookstore, so why get dolled up like a princess or a witch? She put on her gym shoes that had yellow reflectors on the sides and headed out the door.

Aside from a lonely dog barking off in the distance, Fair Haven was quiet. A couple of cars sped away a couple of streets over. Maggie could hear her footsteps along the sidewalk as she approached her car. As she drove alone on the street, seeing the occasional pedestrian jogging across the street or a bike rider stopped at a red light to wait for Maggie to drive past, she wondered if it might not be a bad idea to skirt past Patrick's garage to see if anyone or anything was happening there. She decided against it. He was the kind of man who might set a booby trap. Instead, she made her way to the park as she planned.

There was an allure to parking underneath the streetlamps. How many self-defense instructors advised that this was exactly what every woman should do when venturing out alone? Just about all of them recommended parking in the light.

But Maggie opted for the darkest corner she

could find. Just off an alley was a small section of pitch-black darkness where the light was unable to reach. Her car slipped into the parking spot. After she shut off the engine and flipped the lights, Maggie sat for a moment. She'd been in Fair Haven most of her life. It never ceased to amaze her how different it looked at night. At any second, the shadows would start to slither and skip menacingly around the town, looking to capture something or someone that normally fit nicely into the world of the light.

She took a deep breath before climbing out of the car. Out of habit, she slammed her door shut, making herself jump. The thud echoed and bounced off the surrounding buildings.

"Why not just honk the horns and flash the lights to let everyone know you're here, Mags," she hissed into the darkness. After standing still for a few seconds, waiting for someone or something to emerge from the darkness and zero in on her, she let out a long sigh of relief. The area was still as quiet as a church.

Without waiting, she hurried to the park. Suddenly, she stopped at the entrance. It was even darker in there than it was standing on the sidewalk. She put her hand to her chest and felt her heart beating madly through her sweatshirt. After a couple deep breaths, she steeled her nerves and walked into the darkness.

The temperature dropped several degrees as Maggie felt herself swallowed by the shadows. The place where she stumbled upon Harold Beebe was just down the path and across some grass. At least her ankles weren't exposed to be tickled by the wet grass, and the moisture wasn't soaking through her shoes. But the cool air brushed across the sweat that was forming down the center of her back and up her neck, sending chills throughout her whole body.

As she walked, she listened over her footsteps for anything unusual. It was sudden when she heard the voices. Who was there? It wasn't that she didn't believe Gary that kids congregated at this morbid place, but she'd doubted that she would stumble across any of them. What were the chances that on this night at this time she was actually going to see them? And what was she hoping to find out?

None of that mattered now. She crept up to the nearest thick tree and listened. As her eyes adjusted to the darkness, she could see the glowing tips of cigarettes just ahead of her. Sure enough, it was near the place where Harold Beebe died. Maggie held her breath and crouched down to inch her way closer to the sound of their voices. It didn't take long for the smell of marijuana to hit her nose.

"This was where it happened, yo. We must start at this place. Every time we've been here, the police have showed up. We need to start now," one person said.

"I think we ought to leave this alone. What if…" a female said but was interrupted by another person.

"Sally, if you are scared—"

"I'm not scared. It's just that Malcolm takes so darn long to get the thing going, it's no wonder the cops find us. And do we have to have as many candles as the Sistine Chapel?" she hissed.

"What's the Sistine Chapel?" another person asked.

Are you serious? Maggie thought. She shook her head in disgust.

"Okay. Okay. Let's get started," the first voice said. Maggie squinted, counting five people there. A tiny candle was lit and placed on the ground. They were all sitting around it, except one person was still standing. He was saying something. Maggie was sure she heard the name Lucifer as well as Harold. It didn't take long for one of them to start laughing.

"You're ruining it," one of the males said.

"This is such bull. And what do you expect Harold to do even if you do conjure him? Do you think he's going to bring us some smack from the grave? Look, everyone knows who got him and why. This is just a waste of time." The person who was speaking got up from the circle. "I'm getting out of here."

"No, wait. Don't you want to see what happens?" one of the females asked.

"No."

"Yes, you do. Just sit back down. Let Malcolm try again," she insisted.

"I'm scared," another female added.

"You don't have to be scared," the one who started laughing said. "This isn't real."

"You don't think this is real? It's as real as you want to make it." The one who had been standing and chanting from the beginning sounded offended. "I know what I'm doing. Harold is waiting for us to contact him. He wants to talk to us and tell us he's on the other side."

"Maybe he'll tell us who did him in," one of the females said.

"We all know who did it. And we know why. That was Harold's choice. Now, everybody take a seat around the light, and let's try this again," the leader, Malcolm, instructed. Even the giggler took his place, and all the kids got quiet.

Maggie watched as Malcolm held a lighter to a small book and began mumbling things only his tight little group could hear. The wind kicked up slightly, making the flame of the candle flicker and lick at the darkness as it clung to life. It seemed rather dramatic, yet Maggie couldn't help feeling a shiver run up her spine.

The feeling of the bark beneath Maggie's fingers as she leaned against the tree was rough. An owl hooted off in the distance. The smell of wet, damp earth and concrete from the street mixed when she inhaled deeply through her nose.

"What's that noise?" The female who had admitted to being scared was looking over her shoulder.

"That's the wind," the skeptic of the group said.

"No, I hear someone walking," she insisted.

"Stacy, stop. Now you're scaring me," the other female said.

"I'm telling the truth. I hear someone walking on the grass," Stacy insisted again as she pushed herself off the ground. "I'm not doing this. I'm getting out of here."

"Wait, Stacy. I'll go with you," the skeptic said,

quickly getting off the ground and chasing after her. Malcolm was left with the other girl and a boy who had been quiet the entire time.

"Malcolm?" The other female sounded nervous. Maggie looked all around the grounds, squinting to try to make out all the forms that were in even darker shadows than she was. She could make out the trees, bushes, and benches, and then she saw it. A large form that was pitch-black and making its way toward the group that was still illuminated by the little candle. Her eyes bugged as she watched it almost glide up to them.

"Wh-who is that?" Malcolm tried to appear brave, unshaken, but his voice wavered and gave him away.

A whole line of obscenities came from the dark figure, and Maggie knew instantly who it was. Patrick Cusik. It looked like Malcolm did manage to summon a demon, Maggie thought.

"It's none of your business what we're doing here. What are you doing here?" Malcolm barked with an undeniable relief in his voice that he didn't actually conjure up Lucifer.

"I'm telling you to take your trinkets and your little spell book and get out of here!" Patrick shouted, his voice an abrupt slap across the quiet landscape of the park. Maggie looked over her shoulder to see if his barking had attracted anyone else to the park. But it was as quiet as a graveyard.

"You can't tell us what to do," Malcolm replied as his remaining two friends got up off the ground to stand behind him. Maggie didn't think Malcolm was much of a barrier if Patrick decided to actually put his words into action.

"What did you just say?" Patrick stomped up to Malcolm like he'd done to her more than once. Malcolm took a couple steps back, bumping into his friends, who were also going to be no help if this became physical.

"You can't tell us what to do. Who the heck are you, anyway? Just some perv out creeping in the park after dark, hoping to find some teenagers making out in the bushes. Is that it?" Where Malcolm suddenly got the nerve from, Maggie didn't know. But what he said to Patrick wasn't smart. It was stupid. Suddenly, with lightning speed, Patrick grabbed him by the collar and shook him violently.

"I'm telling you to get out of the park. This is no place for you to be doing your little hexes. Do you understand me? Did my words get through your head?" Patrick hissed.

Malcolm didn't say anything but nodded his head. All of this was unfolding by the romantic light of the one little candle that was still lit and flickering on the ground. Just as Patrick pushed Malcolm back, he kicked over the candle. Everyone was engulfed in almost complete darkness. The streetlights struggled to reach this far into the park, and the solar lights planted around the plaques and signs describing the flowers and who dedicated a bench were too weak to illuminate anything.

Maggie's feet became lead. In the darkness, she clung to the tree she was peeking from and listened.

"You're crazy, mister! Get your hands off me!" Malcolm yelled.

Maggie held her breath and heard the other kids yelling at Patrick to let him go. One of them flipped on a lighter, and when they did, Patrick released Malcolm, thrusting him backward into his friends. It was a split second later that they were returning the obscenities to Patrick as they ran away in the direction Stacy and the skeptic had taken off in.

With everything quiet, Maggie stayed put. She didn't dare start walking and give herself away to the unhinged temper of Fair Haven's angry mechanic. After leaning in closer to the tree, she watched as Patrick snapped on a small flashlight and started shining it all along the ground where the kids had been. He kicked the candle, causing it to splinter and go flying toward the tree she was hiding behind. What was he looking for? Surely the police had collected every bit of evidence from the crime scene that they could. But it didn't change the fact that Patrick was snooping around a crime scene looking for something.

Suddenly, he stopped and stooped down to grab something off the ground. Maggie squinted and tried to focus on what it could be when she felt something hairy and big quickly crawl onto her hand. Of course, if this were the movies, she would have stifled a scream and let the mysterious insect crawl slowly over her hand as sweat dripped down her face and her heart raced. But this was real life. Maggie let out a yelp. Patrick matched it with a high-pitched squeal before shining his flashlight in her direction. By the time the beam of light caught the reflectors on her gym shoes, Maggie was charging toward her car.

"Hey! I see you! Hey! Get back here!" Patrick shouted.

Maggie reached her car, colliding into it as she grunted and gulped at the air. In her mind, she ran like an Olympic gold medalist, her legs stretching elegantly and gracefully as her arms pumped at her sides. In reality, she was a spaz of arms flailing and her legs staggering as she tried to see where each foot was going to land in order to not break an ankle. Although she'd never admit it, she knew she looked more like an ostrich racing across a field of tall grass and dirt.

With a yank, she pulled open her car door then climbed in. She slammed then locked the door, fumbled for her keys in the ignition, and looked in Patrick's direction. She saw the flashlight bobbing up and down as he was in pursuit.

"I didn't think that big lummox would be able to catch up." She panted as she threw the car into gear and sped away. Her heart was pounding, her vision was crystal clear, and her breathing was slowly returning to normal. Although she wasn't sure exactly what she'd seen, she was sure it was something that Gary would be interested in knowing about. He'd be thrilled.

Chapter 17

"What were you thinking, Mags?" Gary ran his hand through his hair then let it fall and slap against his thigh.

"What are you talking about? That guy is a menace, and I think he was up to something. He chased those kids away after he shook one of them like he was nothing more than a rag doll. What's he doing in the park at three thirty in the morning? Tell me that's not the behavior of an oddball," Maggie said.

"Maggie, you were out there too. Yes. That is the behavior of an oddball," Gary said. "I know you've lived here forever. So have I. But walking around by yourself at three in the morning isn't smart in any town, no matter how long you've lived there and think you know everyone."

"So, are you going to question him as to why he was out there?" Maggie huffed and pulled her lips down in a frown. "I'm sure he was looking for something he left behind after he killed Harold Beebe for trying to steal from his shop."

"That isn't what he was doing out there," Gary replied. "I've run into Patrick at least a dozen times when I'm working the night shift. He suffers from insomnia."

"And you believe him?"

"He's been roaming the town at night for months," Gary replied.

"If he's been roaming the town for months, then how come he didn't see anything the night Harold was killed? He didn't hear anything? That sounds very convenient," Maggie replied.

"Maggie, Patrick has been in Fair Haven for almost a decade. Sure, he's rough around the edges, but he's no killer. Now, I want you to promise me that you aren't going to go out traipsing around town in the middle of the night," Gary scolded.

Maggie screwed up her lips before she looked him in the eyes. There was a flicker of worry there for a brief second, but then it was gone and replaced with that stern policeman look. She nodded. Still, she couldn't help feeling that Patrick had something to do with what was going on. He was certainly more of a suspect than Casper was. Although Casper's behavior was also suspicious.

"Gary, I need to tell you something," Maggie said. "I probably should have told you sooner, but I didn't. I was afraid I was jumping the gun."

"What is it?"

Maggie proceeded to tell Gary about Casper's interaction with Harold and Maynard. That they had been waiting for him for several days outside the store and that with each visit, things seemed to escalate. They were pushing him around, and he'd come in with a black eye the day before Harold was found dead.

"I'm sorry I didn't tell you sooner. I just thought there would be something to solidify my gut feeling that Casper had nothing to do with this."

Gary was writing everything down. His face had no expression. There was no kindness in his eyes like there had been just a few short days ago when he took her statement after she'd found Harold's body. Finally, she let out a deep sigh.

"Is there anything else?" he asked.

Maggie shook her head.

"Okay. I'm going to take this to the sheriff. He'll be in touch if he needs anything else," Gary said and turned to leave the bookstore.

"Gary, I'm sorry," Maggie said.

She only got a tired smile and a nod in return. That was worse. It was one thing to have a guy like Patrick not like you. It was another to have someone who had only ever been nice feel like you let them down. Maggie kicked herself for the rest of the day. How could she have been so stupid and not told him everything? She wasn't a detective or a cop. All day at the bookstore, Maggie walked around in a daze, kicking herself for causing Gary to be mad at her.

"Mags, are you all right?" Babs asked when Maggie came in for a cup of coffee. For some reason, the blond woman's cute face made Maggie open up and let her know what she'd done.

"Please don't tell Joshua. He thinks I'm crazy as it is." Maggie wrapped her hands around the warm cup of coffee and took a sip. It was delicious. That made her remember the bitter freeze-dried stuff she gave to Gary when he'd been working so hard. Again, her gut twisted with guilt.

"Well, I think you are crazy too. Gary is right. You could have gotten hurt. A young man stronger and younger than you was stabbed to death. Do you think if you ran into the same person, he'd see you wrinkle your nose and squint adorably and let you go?" Babs asked.

"I don't think that," Maggie replied.

Babs smiled kindly. "You've got a couple of good fellows who care about you here. Don't make them worry. Especially the one in the badge. He won't be able to do his job well if he's always worrying about you."

"Oh no." Maggie huffed. "You don't think he'll be distracted now, do you? What have I done? Gary and I have known each other since high school. If anything happened to him, I'd never forgive myself."

"Calm down. You said he's just going to talk to the sheriff. Let him be," Babs soothed.

"Maybe I should call him?"

"I think it would be better to let that sleeping dog lie. He won't stay gone long. Tell me, how do you feel about Gary?" Babs asked, batting her long black lashes and smirking slightly.

"Why do you ask?"

"No reason. It's just that he seems like the kind of guy a girl would like to have around?" Babs looked down at the napkins she was pulling from a plastic bag to replenish the holders and then peeked at Maggie.

"What guy a girl would like to have around?" Joshua asked as he came in from the back room, pulling off the work gloves he was wearing.

"None of your business," Maggie quipped.

"Gary," Babs said and watched Joshua's reaction with an arched eyebrow.

"Oh. Yeah. Gary is a nice guy. Yeah. I like him," Joshua stuttered and looked at Babs to Maggie and back again. "Um, did I leave a box of nails out here?"

Babs shook her head slowly with a sly grin on her face.

"They must be in the back, and I'm just not seeing them," Joshua said and smiled awkwardly. "I better get back to work. Oh, and the window looks great. I can't believe what you did. I mean, it's really beautiful. Just amazing. Yes. Don't you think, Babs?"

"Yes, Josh. I told her so when I came in this morning," Babs replied. "Roy and Earl were both blown away. Earl can only see the colors, but Roy was impressed. He loves Walter Payton. I just want to know how you came up with such a cool idea. You must really like football."

"She will after the game tomorrow," Joshua said. "I've got everyone's tickets. It's going to be a blast."

Maggie pursed her lips. She didn't want to think about the football game. That was the last thing on her mind. She wanted to know how to make it up to Gary for keeping such important information from him. Without saying another word, she took her coffee into the bookshop. There were people milling around, chatting and looking at the books as she came back in and took her seat at the counter. She smiled and was happy to see some of the copies of old classics move off the shelves, but still, her mind was on Gary.

Casper had showed up for work as if nothing strange had happened at all. He didn't mention running into her at the grocery store, let alone their mutual confrontation with Patrick. Nor did he say anything about leaving her standing outside the store with a box of Ding Dongs in her hand. The fact she had to be marched back inside like a criminal was enough to make her pout her lips and shiver. She'd paid for her snacks while all the evening shoppers watched. It was quite a spectacle.

By the time Maggie locked up the bookshop for the night, she couldn't stand it anymore. She had to go talk to Gary. He didn't call her back or stop in the store to tell her what the sheriff had said or if he went to talk to Maynard about their issue with Casper. So if the mountain wouldn't come to her, she was going to go to the mountain.

After steadying her nerves, she headed off in the direction of the police station. If he wasn't there, Gloria would know where he was. But before she could get there, the screaming siren and rolling red globes of an ambulance caused her to pull to the side of the road. Tailing close behind was Gary in his squad car. She was sure of it. Breaking all kinds of rules of the road, Maggie hit the brakes, backed up over the sidewalk, put the car back in drive, and hit the gas, making the messiest and most illegal U-turn in Fair Haven history. But she followed behind the first responders and realized too late they were heading toward Ricmorris Commons.

Chapter 18

Maggie felt the steering wheel get slick in her hands. She swallowed hard, but her mouth had gone dry. What were the chances of something having happened to someone else at the Commons? Something in her gut told her it was Maynard they were rushing to. Once all the vehicles snaked their way into the parking lot, Maggie found a place to park out of the way and unseen. She quickly got out of the car and watched where the ambulance parked. Sure enough, it was Maynard Ramsey's place.

"Oh no," she muttered as she climbed out of her car. Within seconds, she'd crossed the parking lot and saw Gary get out of his squad car and hurry to the front door of the apartment. There was a woman in her late fifties, maybe early sixties, wearing a tank top and jeans, who was standing to the side of the door crying. She looked rough with skin tinted gray from years of smoking, and it hung loosely around her arms and neck.

The paramedics were the first ones inside the apartment. Maggie's first thought was that Maynard had tried to kill himself. After witnessing the way Sheriff Smith was putting the screws to him, maybe he thought he had no way out of whatever trouble he was in. She wrung her hands as she inched her way up to the scene and blended in with the other neighbors who were gawking at the scene. A couple of other officers from the station, young guys that Maggie didn't know formally but had seen around, were keeping everyone back. Her best bet would be to wait until Gary appeared before trying to get any information.

Instead, Maggie watched the woman at the door who was crying. Was she his mother? Did he live there with that shriveled woman? She might have been pretty at one time, before the elements had mercilessly chipped away at her over the years, removing all the youth and vitality and replacing it with creases in her skin and grime that wouldn't come off. Maggie felt sorry for her.

It was an excruciating amount of time that passed before anyone emerged from the apartment. Gary was the first one. He looked to the woman standing outside the door being comforted by another woman. Maggie didn't hear what he said to her, but from her reaction, it wasn't good. He put his hand on the woman's shoulder, said a little more, and then gave her a business card. He touched her hand gently one more time before turning and heading toward his car while talking into the radio attached to his shoulder. Just as he was about to get in the car, he saw Maggie. He blinked as if he wasn't sure of his own eyes but then, realizing he was seeing clearly, pinched his lips together and came closer.

"What are you doing here?" He didn't look completely mad, but there was a hint of annoyance in his voice.

"I was coming to see you, and you passed me in the opposite direction. So I followed you, and here I am. What happened?" Maggie asked, hoping the situation would be enough to distract Gary from being mad at her.

"Maynard Ramsey is dead. Someone came in and put a bullet to the back of his head. There wasn't anything we could do for him. He's been there about half a day, if I had to guess." Gary wiped his forehead with his hand.

"Oh no. Do you have any leads?"

"That is information for the authorities, Mags. I'm sorry, but none of this is your concern," Gary said. "Please, go home, and don't make me worry about you."

"You don't need to worry about me. I'm a grown woman."

"I know that, Mags. But you aren't a cop. Please, just go home. I've got work to do, and I can't be worrying about you and getting things done right here." Gary gave her a slight smile but didn't say anything else.

Maggie wanted to stand there and argue some more, but now wasn't the time. He was needed, and she was in the way. Fine.

She watched him walk to his car and sit inside behind the wheel, talking into his radio. He was obviously telling Sheriff Smith what had happened. Maggie looked around at the onlookers who were trying to get a glimpse of something gruesome to tell their friends about. That was when she saw him. Hanging back slightly was a tall, lanky-looking young man in a hoodie with a baseball cap. He was intently studying the situation as it unfolded. For a split second, Maggie thought it was Casper. They had the same build, the same look, and Maggie was sure she saw a flash of sandy-brown hair sticking out from beneath his cap. She couldn't be sure unless she got a little closer.

It didn't take long for her to make her way to the right side of the apartment complex, where the young man was looking over the heads of the rest of the crowd that had congregated outside the apartment. There wasn't a single person paying any attention to him. He was like a ghost just floating and hovering around, but Maggie was sure there was something odd about the way he was watching. Like he was waiting for them to discover something else? Maybe he just wanted to make sure the job was done and Maynard was indeed dead.

"Maybe he's just a guy who is morbid and lurking around hoping to see some blood too. Did you ever consider that?" she mumbled.

But as she got closer, she noticed something else about this guy. His gym shoes were white and had a couple red specks on them. They were also the newest style of some designer brand that Maggie had seen on television. A pair of those cost the same as her rent. His jeans were black. His sweat-shirt was black. By this time, Maggie knew he wasn't just a casual observer. He was up to something.

After squaring her shoulders and taking a deep breath, she decided she was going to rush up to this stranger and start asking questions. But before she could make a scene, he locked his eyes with hers. It wasn't Casper. Close, but not him. This man's eyes were nearly black and bore into her so intently that she could barely see the rest of his face. He knew she knew he didn't belong there. It was a glare that stopped her in her tracks and made her tremble.

Before she could even think of what to do next, the young man turned and dashed off between two of the buildings. He was gone, but he'd gotten a good look at her. Maggie stood out like a sore thumb in her cuffed blue jeans with a button-down blouse and cardigan.

"And you got a good look at him, too, Mags," she tried to comfort herself. But it didn't work.

"Maggie! Go home!" Gary shouted from the car. "If I have to tell you again, I'm going to have you arrested for interfering with a crime scene investigation."

Maggie gasped as she whirled around to see not just Gary looking at her but the entire group of rubberneckers. Once again, just like at the grocery store the other night, Maggie was the center of attention for all the wrong reasons. She attempted to say something, but Gary turned his back and marched back into the apartment. Everyone was waiting for Maggie to leave. She felt her cheeks turn red as she turned and walked to her car. Now she'd have to wait to find out all the details of what happened to Maynard.

Even though the strange man watching everything happen stuck in her craw, she didn't think Gary would be in any mood to listen to her. She'd call Gloria at the station and tell her to have Gary contact her immediately once he reported to the station. Maybe the tall, lanky, Casper look-alike was nothing. Maybe it was just a coincidence. Maybe he was just a guy like Patrick Cusik. An oddball in the neighborhood that was harmless, even if they were intimidating looking. Maggie was sure that Gary would come back with some story about this kid, that he was just a guy who likes the flashing lights and shows up at every police call just to watch the red lights roll around in their plastic domes.

Still, Maggie had a weird feeling about the guy. She hurried back to her car and, once inside, locked all the doors. As she pulled away and wove her way back through the apartment complex, she saw him.

He was behind the wheel of a sedan with the windows rolled down. It took him a matter of seconds to catch up to her car and tail her closely. He wasn't honking the horn or speeding up on her. He just followed her as she twisted and turned, hoping to find open road soon. Finally, when she got to the street, she hit the gas and sped in the opposite direction of her home. He took off in pursuit. Maggie's Dodge Neon was no match for whatever was under the hood of this guy's car. He easily kept up with her as she tried to turn down the side streets and alleys.

Her first thought was to drive to the police station, but then she remembered that just about every officer was already at Maynard's place. Gloria might be there all alone, and although Maggie was sure she'd be the kind of woman to shoot first and ask questions later, bringing danger right up to the police station door was not what she wanted to do. Plus, it would take this jerk a couple seconds to see where she was leading him. He'd turn tail, and no one would believe that she was being followed. There was only one place to go, and that was the bookstore. Hopefully Joshua was staying at the upstairs apartment. He'd believe her. At least, she hoped he would.

Chapter 19

"He's outside, Joshua. I'm telling you he followed me all the way from Ricmorris Commons," Maggie said as she tried to catch her breath as she sat on the edge of the couch in Joshua's apartment over the bookstore.

She'd normally be able to park her car right in front of the business. But it was still torn up and blocked for the football game. So Maggie had to park where she had been for the past week and dart through the park. This was now the second time she was running, maybe for her life, through that dark, spooky place. It was bad enough she had a stranger following her. But there was the awful chance that Patrick was in the park poking around and might also take off after her. Now she knew what the gazelle felt like when the lions were near.

"Who is following you?" Joshua asked as he brought her a glass of water and then peeked out the curtains at the street. Maggie had made enough noise unlocking the front door and coming into the bookstore to wake up Joshua's father, who was resting peacefully six feet under in St. Luke's cemetery.

"I don't know who he is. But he was at the scene of Maynard Ramsey's death, and he knew I knew he looked suspicious. I was about to go up to him when he took off down a gangway. But once I was in my car and driving away alone, he showed up right behind and followed me. I parked the car and took off running in order to get here." Maggie took one deep, long breath and let it out slowly before sipping her water.

"What kind of car was he driving?"

"A sedan with tinted windows," Maggie replied.

"Did you get a license plate number?" Joshua asked.

"No. But I bet he was the guy that Gary was talking about who someone reported seeing throwing a knife into Hickory Creek. According to Gary, the person fit Casper's description. Well, had

I not gotten up close enough at this latest crime scene, I would have thought it was Casper too."

When she'd barged into the bookstore, setting off the jingling bells before slamming the door shut, Joshua had been in the upstairs apartment relaxing in front of the vintage fireplace with the television on. He came stomping downstairs in his jeans and a tight-fitting T-shirt. His feet were bare, and he had a five-o'clock shadow like Gary had had the previous night when everyone seemed to be up past their bedtime.

"You still aren't making any sense, Mags. If you were being followed, why didn't you drive to the police?" Joshua asked.

"Because then no one would believe me," Maggie replied.

"What do you mean? Of course they would have," Joshua said as he looked out the window again. "I don't see any... wait."

Maggie held her breath. Joshua waved her to the window. She quickly got up and peeked out the curtain. Down on the street was the sedan that had been following her.

"That's him. That's the same car," Maggie whispered as if the driver might hear her.

"I'm going to call the police," Joshua said.

"And tell them what? That a strange car is slowly driving past the…" Just then, there was the sound of shattering glass and the squeal of tires. Within an instant, the car was gone. Maggie followed Joshua downstairs to find a couple of rocks on the floor surrounded by broken glass in the café.

"Oh, Joshua. This is my fault. I'm so sorry," she said as tears filled her eyes. The painting she'd done on the glass was ruined. The floor was a mess, and now Joshua was going to have to pay to have plywood put up and the glass replaced.

"It's all right," Joshua said.

"You can take it out of my paycheck," Maggie blubbered. "It's all my fault. I'll pay for it."

"It isn't your fault, Maggie. You aren't responsible for what someone else does," Joshua said as he stooped to look at the damage and inspect the windows.

"Gary was right. If I would have just kept my nose out of everyone else's business. Oh my gosh! Patrick was right too. He said I stuck my nose where it didn't belong. Now look what I've done."

"Who's Patrick?"

"I've made a mess of everything."

"No, Maggie. Don't cry. This is just stuff. I have

insurance. Come on," Joshua said as he walked over and hugged her tightly. "It's all right."

Maggie leaned into his chest and cried. She couldn't help it. She was scared and worried and annoyed all at once. She was the person who had come across Harold Beebe's body first. How was she supposed to cope with the shock other than digging to find out what had happened to him? If she just sat around, the memory of his bloody body and staring eyes would stay in her head for months, if not longer. She'd end up at Little Al's Place as a permanent fixture, trying to drink the image of Harold Beebe out of her head.

When she felt Joshua squeeze her tightly, she took a deep breath and let it out slowly. She had one arm at her side and the other against his chest. His heart was beating fast. Before she could look up to him, she felt him kiss her tenderly on the top of her head. Now her heart was beating fast. What was she supposed to do? She knew what she wanted to do. She wanted to look up into his eyes, pull him close, and kiss him on the lips. But she didn't dare. He was her boss. The window of his café had just been shattered by some thug who might have been a murderer. It was no time for romance. Maggie reluctantly pushed back and pretended she hadn't felt his kiss.

"Let me call the police and get these windows boarded. Then I'll take you home," Joshua said as he went to the phone.

"No. I can make it home myself," she insisted.

"Right. Walk through the park alone. You said you parked your car and had to run here. There's no telling what he might have done to your car. Or he might just be waiting for you. No. I'll take you home. Just resign yourself to the fact that you are going to have to wait until I get all this taken care of," Joshua ordered as he pulled a chair from beneath one of the café tables, patted the seat, and held it out for Maggie. She sat down, wiped her eyes, and folded her hands in her lap. He was right. She decided to listen to him for a change.

Chapter 20

By the time the café was secured, Joshua had called the insurance agency as well as a friend he knew in the window business who would be by first thing in the morning to give him a quote. It was almost twelve o'clock when she and Joshua headed to Maggie's home.

"I don't think I ever rode in your car before," Maggie said as she yawned.

"I can tell it's thrilling you," Joshua teased.

"I'm tired. It's been a long day. I still need to talk to Gary, but I'm sure his hands are full. He said since the influx of visitors that there's been a lot more trouble, so he's been working late," Maggie said.

"What's the deal with you two?" Joshua asked.

"What do you mean?"

"I'm just asking. He seems to be comfortable around you. Like maybe you guys have some kind of history together," Joshua said.

"Gary and I went to high school together. We've known each other for years," Maggie said. "What are you getting at?"

"Nothing. I was just asking."

"Did Gary say something to you?"

"No, Mags. He didn't say anything at all," Joshua replied.

"Because I should know if he's talking about me," she said just before yawning again.

"I think you are overtired," Joshua said as he drove toward Mrs. Peacock's home. "You are in no condition to drive. I don't want you falling asleep at the wheel."

"I'm not that tired," she fussed.

"Maybe not, but we aren't taking any chances. I'm taking you home. We'll check out your car tomorrow when the sun is up and there are more people around. For all we know, he didn't do anything. But I'm not taking any chances with you." Joshua made it sound like that was the end of the conversation, so Maggie concurred.

But as Joshua wound around the subdivision

where Mrs. Peacock lived, he and Maggie were both startled to find Sheriff Smith's car already in the driveway.

"Oh my gosh. I hope Mrs. Peacock is all right," Maggie said and sat up straight in the passenger's seat. If another one of her friends got hurt because of her, she was just going to fold herself up in a box and ship herself to Borneo.

"I see Mrs. Peacock in the doorway," Joshua said as if he were reading Maggie's thoughts. She did let out a sigh of relief as Joshua pulled in next to the sheriff's car.

"Are you all right?" Maggie shouted as she quickly scuttled out of the car. "Did something happen?"

"What are you talking about?" Mrs. Peacock looked at Maggie as if she suspected she might be drunk. Again. It hadn't escaped the landlady's notice the night Maggie came home inebriated. Maggie was given a stern talking-to that a drink occasionally was fine and enjoyable, but coming home downright drunk was a bad habit to start. Although Maggie tried to explain to her landlord that this was a onetime incident, she could tell that Mrs. Peacock would have loved if there were more juicy details surrounding Maggie's act of poor judgment. Admitting she had no idea what a shot was or what Wild Turkey was just didn't sound scandalous enough. So the issue was dropped.

"Maggie Bell, just the person I wanted to talk to," Sheriff Smith said. Even when the man said good morning or sang happy birthday, he was still intimidating. Maggie had no idea by his expression if he was mad or concerned.

"What can I do for you, Sheriff?" Maggie slowed her steps and nearly caused Joshua to bump into her from behind.

"Good evening, Joshua. I'm glad you are here too." Sheriff Smith adjusted his belt and turned to face them both with his little notebook in his hand. "What can you tell me about your new employee?"

"Babs?" Joshua asked.

"I think he means Casper," Maggie whispered.

"Yes, Casper Lahey. What can you tell me about him?" the sheriff asked and poised himself like a secretary ready to take dictation.

"He's a good worker. Always on time. Does whatever I ask. Right, Maggie?"

"Yes," Maggie said and squinted at the sheriff. She couldn't help but look at Mrs. Peacock, who was waiting with bated breath for anything that might be worth repeating over the grapevine. Just the fact that the sheriff was at her doorstep looking for her tenant was enough to get the gossip flowing.

"Do you know where he lives? Does he have any family here? Any friends he's mentioned?" Sheriff Smith asked and looked at Maggie. Hadn't he already talked with Gary? Didn't he tell him about the incidents she'd seen with Harold and Maynard?

"You talk to him more than I do, Mags," Joshua said innocently enough. But Maggie didn't like the spotlight being put on her. She stuttered and cleared her throat before telling Sheriff Smith the same things she told Gary.

"But now Maynard Ramsey is dead," Maggie said. "Whoever killed Harold Beebe probably killed him too. And there was a guy there at the Ricmorris Commons who looked just like Casper. But it wasn't him. I know it wasn't."

"Margaret Bell, you seem to know a lot about what is going on in this town. How do you know about Maynard Ramsey?" The sheriff looked at her intently, like he was trying to see through her. The memory of seeing him give Maynard a verbal beating the other day flashed in front of her eyes. She didn't dare breathe a word that she'd seen it.

"I… was going to talk to Gary to apologize, and he passed me heading in the opposite direction with the lights and siren on, so… I decided… to follow him?" She pouted her lips and wrinkled her nose.

Sheriff Smith took a deep breath and let it out, shaking his big bald head as he scribbled in his notepad.

"And there was a guy there who looked like Casper, but it wasn't him. I'm positive it wasn't him. He was just sort of hanging back from the crowd. Like he wanted to see how everyone was going to respond to the murder. I think he had something to do with it," Maggie said. "Then, he followed me all the way back to the bookstore. He broke the windows on the café. Right, Joshua?"

"The windows did get broken, and Maggie said the car that drove by was the one that was following her," he replied.

"Neither one of you have told me where Casper lives. I need to talk to him. He could be in trouble too," Sheriff Smith said.

Maggie shrugged her shoulders and looked at Joshua.

"I'm sorry, Sheriff. When I hired Casper, he said he was staying at a friend's house while he waited for his background check for a new apartment to be done. I didn't think anything of it. In fact, he was such a good employee, I just sort of forgot about following up on that."

"Do you know the name of his friend?" Sheriff Smith asked.

"No, sir," Joshua replied.

"What about you?" He looked at Maggie, who shook her head no. "He never told you anything about his family, friends, where he stays? Nothing?"

"No. In fact, when I tried to make small talk, he told me to mind my own business," Maggie admitted and looked up at Joshua before shrugging her shoulders.

Sheriff Smith didn't say any more. He looked at Maggie and Joshua, and it was like a light went on behind his eyes. "Where was the last place you saw Casper with his car?" he asked.

"Um, he was in the parking lot of the grocery store. Why?" Maggie said.

She also spilled what happened with Patrick at the grocery store. Even if Gary didn't think he was guilty of anything more than insomnia, Maggie thought he deserved a visit from the sheriff just for spite.

The sheriff turned to Mrs. Peacock, who was standing in one of her brilliantly colored muumuus and fuzzy slippers that clapped against her heels when she walked.

"Thank you for your help, Vivian," he said.

"Anytime, Lee," she said as he turned and pushed past Maggie and Joshua.

"Sheriff, is there anything we can do to help?" Maggie asked.

"Maggie, I want you to stay here with Mrs. Peacock in the big house. Don't stay alone in your guesthouse. Joshua, can you follow me?" The sheriff didn't quite ask as much as suggest Joshua go along.

"Of course, Sheriff," he replied and handed Maggie off to Mrs. Peacock.

"Wait a minute. Why do I have to stay with Mrs. Peacock? Why can't I go to my house?" Maggie called after them.

"Vivian, make sure she does what she's told. Maggie, just trust me on this. You might be in trouble. But right now, Casper might be in bigger trouble than you. Stay put. Keep the doors locked, and don't answer for anyone but me or Joshua. Understand?" The sheriff didn't wait for Maggie or Mrs. Peacock to reply. He was already in his car with the light on and the siren going. Joshua was also speeding away behind him without saying a word.

"Come on, dear. Let's do as the sheriff says." Mrs. Peacock guided Maggie by the shoulders into the house.

She shut the front door with a solid thud and slipped two dead bolts and a chain in place. Fort Knox wasn't as secure as Mrs. Peacock's house. At least, that was what Maggie thought at first. It wasn't until she saw the shadows that she began to worry.

Chapter 21

Maggie looked at Mrs. Peacock. "I'm sorry about this. I seem to be a beacon for bad luck these days."

"What are you talking about?" Mrs. Peacock asked in a not-so-subtle way of gathering information. Everyone in town knew Mrs. Peacock was a fount of information. If you wanted a story spread, give it to Mrs. Peacock. Maggie was sure that the Widow Peacock was at the top of the local politicians' lists, as she was better than any flyers or mailings when it came to spreading their often opposing messages.

But Maggie didn't want to seem rude. After all, Mrs. Peacock had no idea what was really going on.

She didn't know about Sandra at Little Al's Place or Patrick at the garage. She was sure she didn't know about the kids trying to conjure up Harold Beebe's spirit in the park. Everything Mrs. Peacock gathered about Maggie from Sheriff Smith was nothing.

"Didn't you ever feel like nothing seemed to go your way?" Maggie said as Mrs. Peacock led them to the kitchen. Her kitchen was as big as Maggie's entire house. It was a magnificent room with soft-yellow paint that was the perfect complement to her white cabinets and white marble countertop. Copper pots hung from a rack over a large island in the middle that was home to the stove and featured a comfortable area to sit at. Maggie climbed up onto one of the stools while Mrs. Peacock grabbed her teakettle and filled it with water.

"Oh, goodness. Of course. When Mr. Peacock passed away, I felt like everything that could go wrong did. I could kill him for dying and leaving me with so many responsibilities and tasks that I knew nothing about. Not to mention the shoestring budget I have to be on," Mrs. Peacock said while looking at the gas flame beneath the kettle. There wasn't a conversation that went by where she didn't mention how strained her bank account was. But everyone knew that Mrs. Peacock was one of the richest people in Fair Haven.

"I don't mean to whine. I'm sorry," Maggie said.

"Don't be silly. Now, tell me, who is Casper, and why was the sheriff asking about him?"

As Maggie watched Mrs. Peacock prepare the tea, she told her how Joshua had hired two new people to help at the café and bookstore. The customer traffic had increased. So had the sales. It was necessary that they hire on some help.

"But as soon as Casper arrived, there was trouble," Maggie confessed.

"He just happened to arrive in town at the craziest time," Mrs. Peacock said. "Had it not been for the football team making such a big splash, this town would be empty like usual. There are so many extra people that some of the neighbors have opened their homes to them. For a fee."

"How come you didn't do that? You've got an extra room," Maggie asked, knowing that Mrs. Peacock had at least three guest rooms standing empty at that moment.

"You just never know with people. Look at all that has happened. Not just one murder but two. My goodness, it makes me think maybe it's time to move. After all, I'm on a shoestring budget. I might be able to get a few dollars for this house, but there is so much work to be done if I was going to sell it. And I'd have to worry about what would happen to you." She rolled her eyes just as the kettle began to whistle. She turned off the burner and poured the water into the cups.

"Once again, I'm in the way," Maggie said.

"It's just such a crazy world we live in. Why, I heard that just down the street there was someone peeping in Mrs. Donovan's window when she was getting ready for bed," Mrs. Peacock said as she adjusted the collar of her dress.

Maggie didn't want to say anything. Mrs. Donovan was in her early seventies and had an unspoken rivalry with Mrs. Peacock for Grand Dame of Fair Haven. The chances that Mrs. Donovan mistook the reflection of the television in her window was more likely than there actually being a Peeping Tom trying to catch her in the act of disrobing.

"That's really something. You will let me know if you plan on moving before the movers arrive, won't you, Mrs. Peacock?" Maggie asked, only half joking. Just then the phone rang before Mrs. Peacock could give an answer. She walked over to the bronze-and-wood vintage phone that hung on the wall.

"Hello?" she said before she looked at Maggie. "Why yes. She is. Just a second, Officer Brookes. Maggie, it's Officer Brookes for you." Mrs. Peacock held out the phone.

Maggie hopped off the barstool and walked over to her then took the phone gingerly in her hand and raised it up to her ear.

"Hi, Gary. How did you know I was here?"

"Maggie, I'm so glad you are safe. I need you to stay put until I get there," Gary replied.

"What's the matter?"

"We've got Casper here at the station. You are in danger. Just stay where you are and…"

"Hello? Gary? Can you hear me?"

"What did he say?" Mrs. Peacock asked just as the lights went out.

"He said—" Maggie swallowed hard—"that I was in danger."

With her heart in her throat, she crossed the kitchen and took Mrs. Peacock by the arm.

"Margaret, what's going on?" Mrs. Peacock asked in a low, calm voice.

"I'm not sure, but Gary is on his way here. There isn't anything to worry about. Maybe the power went out all over the neighborhood," Maggie said as they walked through the dark house to the family room in the back of the house. Almost all of it was windows, and across from Mrs. Peacock's beautifully landscaped yard, the lights of the nearest neighbors were still on.

"Looks like they are still on at the Fergusons," Mrs. Peacock said nervously. "Margaret, I think we need to prepare ourselves."

"What? For what?"

"For battle," Mrs. Peacock said. Before Maggie could stop her landlord, the woman was in a closet near the front foyer.

"Mrs. Peacock. I think we should stick together. Mrs. Peacock…" Maggie hissed. She turned to the windows and tried to see if there was anything moving out in the backyard without giving her own position away. Whatever the old woman was doing in the closet, it required she make a ton of noise. If there was a fear of waking the dead, Mrs. Peacock brushed it aside. She wasn't going to stop whatever it was she was doing just because it was causing a ruckus.

"Mrs. Peacock?"

"Shh!" Mrs. Peacock snapped back. Maggie held her breath and listened. Someone was jiggling the front doorknob. There was no way they would be able to get through the two dead bolts. But there were half a dozen other ways to get into the house. Maggie wanted to ask Mrs. Peacock if anything else was open, but she was afraid to move. Then she heard the scariest sound of all.

"You go ahead and try to get in that door!" Mrs. Peacock shouted before cocking what could only be a shotgun. Nothing else made such a terrifying sound.

"Mrs. Peacock? I didn't know you knew how to shoot a gun," Maggie chirped.

"It's a shotgun, honey. And no one does. I'll ask you to keep this little fact about your landlady to yourself," Mrs. Peacock said.

Maggie found it terribly ironic for the town gossip to be asking her to keep a secret. But since she lived on her property for a very good price and was at this moment petrified, Maggie solemnly swore to take this fact to the grave.

After all this, Maggie's eyes had adjusted to the darkness. She could clearly see Mrs. Peacock and her shotgun. She walked over to the front door and gave it a good, solid smack with her hand. The person messing with the knob stopped, and then everything was silent.

"Mrs. Peacock, maybe you should come in here with me," Maggie whispered. "I'd feel a lot better if we were in the same room and there was no chance of you accidentally shooting me."

"I'm going to go and check the other doors," Mrs. Peacock said like she was about to storm the beaches at Normandy.

"The other doors? How many do you think are open?"

"I don't know. That's why I'm going to check. You stay here," Mrs. Peacock said.

"What? Are you crazy? That's the worst idea. You know what happens in the movies when people split up. It never has a good outcome. No way. I'm coming with you." Maggie was about to inch her way to Mrs. Peacock when movement outside in the yard caught her eye.

She froze as the blood in her veins turned to ice.

"Stay where you are, Maggie. He doesn't see me," Mrs. Peacock whispered.

"I can't move," Maggie said.

She stood next to Mrs. Peacock's chaise lounge that was next to the sliding glass door. Thankfully, Mrs. Peacock had a bar along the bottom of the track to prevent the door from being opened. But that didn't stop the hooded character from slowly creeping across the lawn like a pool of black ink spilling over the grass. It was the hooded man from Ricmorris Commons. Had Maggie not known better, she would have thought it was Casper. But she could tell those cold, hard eyes that she stared into at Maynard Ramsey's crime scene were scanning the windows, looking for a way into the house. This meant that he'd followed her from the shop and knew that Sheriff Smith and Joshua had left her there.

How long had he been following her? Maybe he knew her comings and goings for several days. With all the foot traffic and unfamiliar faces in the bookstore, maybe he'd been in there, sizing her up and waiting for an opportunity to strike. All these thoughts made her sick to her stomach. But what made her body tremble was the knife that glinted in his hand as he approached the window. It glinted in the light from the neighbor's house, a cold silver streak that Maggie was sure was a butcher knife no different than the one in Mrs. Peacock's kitchen.

Her mind was telling her to run and hide, but her feet wouldn't move. She stood there like a rabbit hoping the wolf creeping closer wouldn't notice her. But it did. The hooded man stopped in his tracks and pulled his hood back just enough for Maggie to see the black shadows where his eyes were. They stared at one another for what felt like minutes when it was probably only a couple of seconds before Mrs. Peacock calmly and quietly walked up behind Maggie and pointed her shotgun in the man's direction.

"Don't worry, Maggie. He won't try anything," Mrs. Peacock said, but Maggie could see the barrel of the gun shaking. This was no way for a woman her age to be spending her evening.

As if to say he didn't believe her, the man walked up to the sliding door and began to tug at the handle. He tapped on the glass with the knife.

"I see you," he said through the glass. His voice was deep and cold.

"What do you want?" Maggie shouted, her voice cracking nervously.

"Don't act like you don't know," he taunted.

"I haven't the slightest," Maggie insisted. "Mrs. Peacock, do you know what he's talking about? No one knows what you're talking about. Why don't you just move along."

"You're holding it for Casper. I'll deal with him soon enough. But you've got a chance to save yourself and the old lady," the hooded man said with a sinister grin on his face. "Just hand it over, and I'll be on my way."

"What's he talking about?" Mrs. Peacock asked.

"I still don't know what you are talking about. Maybe you're at the wrong house. Try next door. Cut their electricity and phone and see what happens!" Maggie shouted, noticing some of the feeling had come back into her legs, which had seemed to grow roots into the floor. "I don't even know who you are. How can I hand anything over? And even if I did, what guarantee do I have that you'll keep your word? See, that doesn't make sense. You'd have every reason to get rid of us. We'd be able to give the police a partial description. You couldn't risk that. See what I mean? So, you aren't being truthful when you say you just want your stuff, whatever your stuff is."

"Give me my stuff!" he screamed and pounded on the glass, making Maggie and Mrs. Peacock jump. Thankfully, Mrs. Peacock didn't accidentally squeeze the trigger and blow a hole through the glass and the man on the other side of it. He continued to pound and shout at the women, making Maggie back up a few inches with Mrs. Peacock.

"There is no need for me to pull the trigger while he's out there and we're in here," she said as the real possibility of having to pull the trigger began to settle over the room like a fog over a field of tall grass. It permeated everything. The fact that Maggie might witness her landlady actually take a life was more terrifying than the man outside. If Mrs. Peacock's hand was forced, that would mean death and destruction. It would mean she'd be arrested. It would mean that Mrs. Peacock would be the talk of the town for months on end. It was something neither Maggie nor Mrs. Peacock wanted to do or were even prepared to do. And the hooded man knew this, so he kept pounding and yanking at the door.

"He won't get through the glass like that," Mrs. Peacock whispered.

As if he read her lips, the man turned around and dashed off into the darkness for a second. He reemerged from the darkness with a rock he'd taken from Mrs. Peacock's garden.

He hoisted it up over his shoulder. Just as he was about to lob it into Mrs. Peacock's beautiful sliding glass door, there was another noise. For a minute, Maggie's greatest fear, that there was more than one guy outside, seized hold of her heart. But the voice was familiar.

"Freeze! Drop it!" It was Gary. Maggie let out her breath that she hadn't realized she was holding. She put one hand gently on Mrs. Peacock's arm and carefully had her lower the barrel of the shotgun. The hooded man looked to his left, shifted his stance, and threw the rock at Gary.

"Drop the knife! Put your hands over your head! Do it now!" Gary shouted. But his commands fell on deaf ears.

"Why isn't he listening? Why isn't he doing what Gary says?" Maggie clicked her tongue as they watched the scene unfold. This man knew that Gary didn't want to shoot any more than Mrs. Peacock did. It was a sickening display to watch someone with a heart of stone take advantage of someone who knew the meaning of compassion.

"Let's go," Mrs. Peacock said, her shotgun in one hand and Maggie's hand in the other.

"Go where?"

"Anywhere, Margaret. Gary can't do his job if he is worrying about us," Mrs. Peacock said and pulled Maggie toward the kitchen and out of sight. Just then, Maggie heard Gary shout again. He was frantic, screaming commands that were not being followed. There was a single pop from Gary's gun.

Maggie pulled away and ran to the sliding-door

window just in time to see both men running into the shadows. It was dark. All Maggie could think was that Gary might need her help. What if the hooded man got the jump on him? What if he dropped his gun or tripped and hurt his ankle? A million scenarios went through Maggie's head as she stood there frozen in place, trying to figure out what to do.

It was the flash she saw before the sound hit her that made her heart stop. It was like it happened in slow motion. In the trees behind Mrs. Peacock's house not far from Maggie's small cottage, there was a flash of white light for a split second coming from the barrel of a pistol. It wasn't huge. It wasn't like in the movies with exploding sounds and blinding light. It was like someone tossed a single firecracker into the darkness, and its power was seen in that one burst.

Maggie kicked the bar away from the track and yanked the sliding door open. She stepped out onto the patio and listened. There was grunting and growling and leaves and branches being kicked up and crushed. Maggie couldn't see where they were. She didn't know what direction to go or if she should venture out that way.

"Maggie!" Mrs. Peacock hissed. "Maggie, get back inside!"

"Gary is in trouble," she argued.

"Gary is a trained professional. Let him do his job."

"But, Mrs. Peacock, this is my fault. He wouldn't be in this position if I'd been honest with him about what I knew. He's been my friend for so long. If anything happened... what would I do without..."

Just then, a dark form emerged from the tree line. It was just like the pool of ink that had crossed the yard just a short while ago. Maggie's mouth had gone bone-dry. It was the hooded man. That meant Gary was somewhere in those trees, hurt, maybe even dying. And now she was alone to face this monster without him.

"Maggie, get back in the house." She heard Gary's voice but didn't see him.

"What?"

"Get back in the house, Mags. I've got this." From behind the dark hooded shadow was another silhouette that Maggie instantly recognized. To her shock, Gary was escorting the hooded man out of the brambles.

"Oh. Thank goodness." Maggie squinted and

wrung her hands together as she calmly walked back to the house where Mrs. Peacock was waiting in the doorway.

"Gary's got him," Maggie said, glad the lights were off so no one would see she had tears in her eyes.

Chapter 22

It didn't take long for the paramedics to arrive, along with the electric company and the phone company, making the street in front of Mrs. Peacock's home look like the set of a big-budget Hollywood movie.

"I still don't know why you called the paramedics," Maggie said to Gary as she sat on the bumper of his squad car with a blanket around her. Gary stood next to her.

"It's protocol. I shot him," Gary replied.

"You didn't shoot him. You sent a warning shot across the bow, and he got a scrape across his shoulder. Had he done what he intended with the rock from Mrs. Peacock's garden, he wouldn't be getting a Band-Aid put on like he is now. The coroner would be here."

"I'm glad it didn't come to that. Mrs. Peacock is too good of a lady to have that on her conscience," Gary replied.

"Oh, and I promised her I wouldn't tell anyone she had that shotgun. So, mum's the word," Maggie said as she put her index finger to her lips.

"I'm not saying a word," Gary responded. Just then, one of the paramedics came sauntering up to Gary. She was petite with a ponytail and was peeling off her purple latex gloves as she approached.

"You can take him now, Officer Brookes. He doesn't need to go to the hospital. He had a couple of scratches but absolutely nothing life-threatening. He's got a real attitude too. I don't envy you."

"Thanks, Katie." Gary nodded as he watched the woman walk back to the ambulance.

The hooded man was handcuffed to the gurney that was chained to a fixture in the back of the ambulance, which was used for any injured parties who might be on drugs or who might be violent or dangerous like the hooded man was. Gary looked at Maggie.

"Can you meet me at the station?" he asked

with a grin.

"My car is at the bookshop." She frowned, but no sooner had she said the words than Mrs. Peacock emerged from her house, dressed in an expensive tracksuit and gym shoes that looked as if they'd never been worn.

"Margaret, you'll come with me. We'll meet you at the station, Gary. Oh, will you look at all this commotion? I'll be putting out the fires of gossip for weeks. Mrs. Donovan is going to think I had a heart attack or slipped getting out of the tub. Come on, young lady," she said as she went to her Cadillac that was sitting in the driveway.

Maggie would once again hear the story of how Mrs. Peacock's late husband insisted she have this car, and that even though insurance was through the roof and it guzzled gas, she couldn't part with it.

"Yes, ma'am," Maggie replied and looked at Gary. "What happened in the woods, Gary? How did you get him?"

"I fired a warning shot. He didn't think I'd do it. When it grazed him, he lost his balance, and I pounced. Simple by-the-book training. I knew Mrs. Peacock's property sloped a good bit just behind the tree line. Our friend didn't. It pays to know your surroundings." Gary winked.

"I guess it does." Maggie smiled back.

She joined Mrs. Peacock and, as predicted, heard all about how much her late husband spent on the car, how he always wanted to make her happy no matter what, and that now it was draining her bank account. Still, she didn't dare part with it.

"No. Mr. Peacock would be spinning in his grave if I ever got rid of this car. He loved it. Even though people think you have a lot of money if you drive one, I am barely getting by," she said and cleared her throat as they pulled into the police station parking lot.

"Did he buy you the shotgun too?" Maggie asked with her voice lowered like there might be someone eavesdropping or a bug recording their words.

"Nope. I bought that myself." Mrs. Peacock looked at Maggie with a sly smirk. Maggie smiled back. Mrs. Peacock was like a superhero with two distinct sides to her. But like a good sidekick in this particular instance, Maggie promised not to tell about her landlady's double-barrel superpower.

When she got out of the car, Maggie was relieved to see Sheriff Smith's car as well as Joshua's car parked there too. Gary was pulling the hooded man out from the back seat. His head was no longer covered, and from a distance, his resemblance to Casper was spot-on. Poor Casper came to Fair Haven only to have problems right off the bat.

Gary went into the station first. When Maggie walked in, she gasped.

"Casper, what are you doing here?" she asked, her eyes wide.

"Hi, Maggie," he said as he sat in the seat next to Gary's desk. Maggie looked at Joshua, who stood by the coffee machine with his arms folded over his chest and a sly smirk on his lips.

"Joshua, did you report Casper to the sheriff?" Maggie marched up to her boss and stood glaring at him toe-to-toe. "I'm telling you, he had nothing to do with Harold or Maynard's death. Not a thing."

"Do you think I don't know that?" Joshua looked down at her with a smirk.

"Then what is he doing here? What are they holding you here for, Casper?" Maggie demanded and walked up to her coworker.

"Margaret Bell, I think you need to settle down and take a seat. I'd like to introduce you to Casper Lahey," Sheriff Smith said as he emerged from his office.

"I know exactly who he is, Sheriff, and I know he didn't do any of the stuff you think he did. He didn't kill anyone. Go on and tell them you didn't kill anyone," Maggie said after poking Casper in the shoulder.

"Margaret, stop abusing that boy. We know he didn't kill anyone," the sheriff yawped.

It was then that Gary slammed the gate shut on the holding cell that was in the corner, and the hooded man stood there staring daggers at the entire room.

"Maggie, meet Lawrence Tyre. Lawrence, would you like to tell the nice young lady what we've got you here for? And what you thought she had?" Gary needled.

"I want to talk to my lawyer," Lawrence spat.

"Oh, come on. You don't want to brag a little like you were doing before when you were selling those drugs to the teenagers in Odell? You don't want to tell how you made an example of Harold Beebe to your crew? Not interested in singing that song anymore. Too bad." Gary snickered.

"I want my lawyer," Lawrence said through clenched teeth.

"Settle down, Larry," Gary replied as he walked away.

"I don't know what's going on. This isn't making any sense to me," Maggie said and looked at the clock. She couldn't believe it was almost midnight. She felt like she'd been on the move for three days straight.

"Mags, I need to take a statement of what happened tonight," Gary said.

"Are you going to let Casper go?"

"No, Casper is staying with us a little while longer. He hasn't finished giving his statement," Gary replied.

"But he'll be in for work tomorrow, after you look at that new apartment, right, Casper?" Joshua said with a smile.

Casper, who was so shy already, flipped his hair to the right and smiled the biggest smile Maggie had ever seen since he started. Whatever was going on, Casper was no longer in danger. That was a relief. It also meant that Maggie's judge of character was not skewed or faulty. She'd thought he was the right kid for the job, and that proved to be true too. Sure, it was a little self-absorbed to focus on how this all reflected on her. But Maggie had to be able to trust her own judgment, or what else did she have? What did that say about her crush on Gary? Wait, it wasn't Gary she had a crush on. It was Joshua. Wasn't it? She looked at both men, her eyes bouncing from one to the other, and felt a knot tie up in her stomach. She'd known Gary half her life. Joshua was her boss. If she got tangled up with either one of them, it would spell certain disaster.

Maggie bit her tongue and then proceeded to answer the questions Gary asked, describing the events of the night. Mrs. Peacock was next and glared at Lawrence with every word she said as she provided extensive details about the threatening young man who was out to do her and Maggie harm.

Finally, when they were done, Maggie yawned and followed Joshua outside. Mrs. Peacock had a few words for Sheriff Smith and remained in the station for a short while, and Gary had to tend to Casper and their guest of the state.

"I don't get any of this. Why did Lawrence come after me? I don't know him, and I barely know Casper," Maggie said.

"Sheriff Smith told me everything. Lawrence had been a penny-ante thug for some time in and around Fair Haven and some of the other towns, but the police couldn't get anyone to confirm what he was doing. Everyone was afraid of him and rightfully so. Harold and Maynard worked for him, and I use that term loosely. What they did was scare people, young people, into doing their dirty work," Joshua said.

"I didn't think Casper was a bad kid," Maggie said.

"Are you kidding? Casper is amazing. When he showed up here in town, we thought he was just a kid looking for a job. Casper had been living out of his car for the past six months," Joshua said.

"What?" Maggie put her hands to her heart.

"He'd just turned eighteen and got out of a bad situation at his home. Some kids living that kind of existence will quickly fall in with a bad crowd just to feel a sense of community, a sense of family. But Casper was different," Joshua said and shook his head.

"Oh, that poor kid. No wonder he didn't want me asking about his personal life or walking him to his car. Why didn't he say something? We wouldn't have judged him," Maggie said.

"Of course we wouldn't have. But he didn't know that. All he knew was that he needed real work to get settled. But sadly, he ran into Harold and Maynard before he came to the café. They basically handed him a bag of dope and told him to either buy it, sell it, or else. Well, Casper did the only thing he could think of. He went to Sheriff

Smith and told him what had happened and that he had over five thousand dollars' worth of drugs in his car," Joshua said. With every word, Maggie's eyes got wider and wider.

"Oh my gosh. Casper is just a kid. To have this kind of burden had to be horrible. Not to mention terrifying. What did the sheriff do?" Maggie asked, feeling like she was listening to an old-time radio show that was about to resolve the most exciting cliff-hanger in the history of cliff-hangers.

"He made Casper a deal. He told him to say he sold the drugs and that he'd give him the money provided by the police department. Except Fair Haven doesn't have that kind of cash on hand. The sheriff needed to get ten thousand dollars from the state, and that took longer than it was supposed to. That's why Harold and Maynard were hassling Casper. They thought he was holding out," Joshua explained.

"Wow. Real drug dealers right here in Fair Haven. Quite frankly, I'm shocked." Maggie wrinkled her nose and put her hands on her hips.

"That's not surprising. Let's face it. You live on Mrs. Peacock's property. I've got the shop and a small place on the outskirts of town that's quiet and clean. But not all of Fair Haven is a slice of

Mayberry," Joshua said, making reference to the peaceful town in the old black-and-white television show with Andy Griffith as the local sheriff who never had any need for bullets in his pistol.

"But I don't understand. Why did the sheriff want Casper to pretend he sold the drugs?" Maggie asked.

"You've seen those undercover cop movies. If Casper could confirm that it was Lawrence doing the distributing, they could bust him and maybe get higher up the food chain. But it didn't work out that way," Joshua said as he opened the passenger-side door for Maggie.

"What happened?"

"When Harold and Maynard beat Casper up, Casper snapped. He'd been crawling his whole life and just couldn't take it anymore. So, he broke into Maynard's apartment and tossed the money and remaining drugs inside. It was how he cut his hand," Joshua said. "He was going to take his chances, but he was not going to be afraid anymore."

"I still don't understand. If they had their drugs and money back, Lawrence should have been happy. Right?" Maggie sat down in the passenger's seat of the car and watched as Joshua shut the door, walked around, and got in behind the wheel. He started the engine, put the car into gear, and began to drive in the direction of Maggie's home.

"I don't think there is such a thing as a happy drug dealer." Joshua chuckled.

"Maybe you are right," Maggie said and laughed too.

"I'm not sure what transpired between Harold and Lawrence. Whatever it was, Lawrence was not taking it lying down. From what Sheriff Smith said, Lawrence lured Harold to the park and stabbed him to death. He left the body in a place where everyone would see it, and those who didn't see it definitely heard about it. What he didn't bank on was that his action would backfire," he said.

Joshua seemed to be driving extra slow considering there was virtually no one on the road. Maggie was sure it was so he could tell her all the details about the situation.

"How did it backfire?" Maggie asked.

"Maynard was nothing but a coward who liked to talk the talk. But when it came to actually walking the walk, he turned on Lawrence without hesitation. The problem with dealing with cowards is that they can't be trusted at all once you figure out they are cowards."

Now the conversation Sheriff Smith had with Maynard that Maggie overheard made sense. According to Joshua, the sheriff made a similar deal with Maynard to turn the tables on Lawrence. The only problem was that Lawrence had been watching Maynard's apartment. That was how he knew about Maggie. But Maggie didn't tell anyone she'd been at Maynard's apartment or that she'd seen the sheriff and him together.

It made no difference. It was when Maggie followed Gary to the Ricmorris Commons that she faced Lawrence. It was only her crude detective skills that led her to believe he was a strange character who was out of place among the locals.

"For some reason, since you were at the place where Maynard was found, Lawrence thought you had his dope and money. The truth was the sheriff had all of it. It was safe and sound in the police station evidence room." Joshua clicked his tongue.

"The police station has an evidence room?"

"It does. It isn't very big. I think it has evidence from this case and maybe one more from a liquor store robbery a couple years ago." Joshua chuckled. "It's really nothing more than a closet." Maggie giggled.

Joshua continued, "So that was all the sheriff

told me. He wanted my help finding Casper because he was afraid that if Lawrence got to him first, he'd be right back at square one. A dope dealer on the loose who was made of Teflon. No matter what, nothing would stick to him." He shook his head.

"And that's how you found out Casper was living in his car?" Maggie asked softly, as if the words might not be so sad if she didn't speak too loudly.

"Yup. He'd been living in it for about four months. He used the gas station bathroom to wash up. He only had a couple of shirts and jeans that he'd wash at the laundromat. I hate to say it, but he ate what he could find," Joshua said. For a few minutes, they rode in silence. There was nothing either one of them could say that would adequately convey their feelings for what Casper had gone through.

"Well, there has got to be something we can do. He's got to have a place to stay." Maggie tapped her chin. "I'm not trying to make a bad joke, but the Ricmorris Commons has always got a vacancy." Maggie shrugged.

"I can do you one better," Joshua said and looked at Maggie. "I offered him the cottage I was renting on the outskirts of town, and I'll stay in my father's apartment. Permanently."

"What did he say when you did that?"

"He started to cry. I told him it was paid up through the next two months. After that, it would be his responsibility," Joshua replied. "I thought of letting him stay over the bookstore, but something didn't feel right. I just didn't like the idea of anyone else being in my dad's place. I like it there. I feel closer to him. I was thinking of expanding the bookstore to include a second floor, but I think we might just acquire the building on the other side instead." Joshua smiled, but Maggie saw the tears glisten in his eyes. She looked ahead to the road.

"That was a nice thing you did." She squinted.

"You think so?"

"Yeah. I think so," Maggie replied. "For Casper and for your dad."

"Thanks, Mags."

"You're welcome, Joshua."

"You want to stop at Little Al's Place for a drink?"

Maggie put both hands to her throat, making gagging noises as Joshua laughed.

Chapter 23

Mrs. Peacock was happy to drive Maggie to work the following morning. The entire town was abuzz with not only the news of the young man Lawrence Tyre trying to break into the widow Vivian Peacock's house while she was home, entertaining her female tenant who lived in the guest cottage behind the main house, but also the excitement of the football game taking place that afternoon.

As they approached the café, Maggie was surprised to see Gary already there and the huge lumbering shape of Patrick standing with him in front of her car that looked like it had been washed. Gary shook Patrick's hand before the goliath turned and walked down the street a few steps before he climbed into the dented-up SUV she'd seen him in at the grocery store.

Mrs. Peacock pulled up in front of the café. "I'm going to park down the street a way, and then I'll be in for a cup of coffee."

"Okay. I'll have one ready for you. Thanks again for the ride, Mrs. Peacock."

"I can't have you sitting around just because your car is down here. If you have a job to go to, you need to go to it. I'm not running a charity. I need that rent money, and I need it on time," Mrs. Peacock replied while looking straight ahead.

"Yes, ma'am," Maggie said as she climbed out of the long black Cadillac that everyone in town knew was Mrs. Peacock's. Maggie waved to Gary as she walked up to him.

"Good morning," he said before yawning.

"Did you pull another all-nighter?" she asked, wrinkling her nose.

"Yeah, it took a while to get Mr. Tyre tucked in for the night and make sure his babysitters were on time to take him to county this morning," Gary said with the satisfied look of a man who put in his time and got the job done.

"What were you talking to the Jolly Green Giant about?" Maggie asked as she jerked her thumb over her shoulder in the direction Patrick had just left.

"Well, he had your car towed from the other street to here after he checked the oil and had it driven through the car wash," Gary said.

"Why would he do that?" Maggie frowned, her eyes wide.

"I asked him to," Gary said. "He gave me a good price. And he asked when was the last time you had the oil changed. You'll need to bring it in again in three months to keep it in good shape. I'll remind you."

"I don't have to take it in to him, do I?" Maggie asked as if she was just told in order to get her keys, she'd have to reach into a fish tank full of tarantulas.

"No, Mags. You can go anywhere you like." Gary smirked. "That little matchbox looks nice when it's clean. You might want to keep it washed too. I'm just saying."

"Thank you for paying for the oil change. I'm normally pretty good at staying on top of things, but with the shop being so much busier all the time and only now getting some help, I guess I just forgot about it. I'll pay you back," she muttered then looked up at Gary. He had that handsome five-o'clock shadow again, and there was a twinkle in his eyes.

"Yeah. You will." He winked. "I've got to get home, or I'm going to fall asleep in this doorway standing up straight like a horse does. Your landlord is still around, looking in her element."

Maggie turned around. It was true. Instead of driving away, Mrs. Peacock was chatting up a storm with none other than the notorious Mrs. Donovan, telling her all the gory details about the previous evening's excitement. Minus the shotgun, of course.

"It was absolutely terrifying," Mrs. Peacock was saying. "I just don't know what I would have done had Officer Brookes not shown up when he did. Officer! I can't thank you enough for everything you did last night. I do hope Sheriff Smith knows how lucky he is to have you on the force."

"It's part of the job, Mrs. Peacock. Don't mention it."

"Oh, I will mention it. I'll be mentioning it to everyone in town," the Widow Peacock replied as she pulled the door to the café open and stepped inside with Mrs. Donovan following.

"Vivian, I am just shocked. I shudder to think of what might have happened had he gotten into your home. You really should think of a home security system or maybe even… a gun," Mrs. Donovan whispered.

"Maybe you are right, Tabitha. I just don't know how I'll recover from this. The only thing that brings me any comfort is that I have a tenant on the property. Even if it is only Margaret Bell," Mrs. Peacock said as she stepped inside the café.

Maggie twisted her mouth to the side and looked at Gary. They both chuckled but said nothing else. Gary went to his squad car. Maggie went into the bookstore. As she stashed her purse behind the counter, she could hear the café burst into action as Mrs. Peacock drew everyone's attention.

"Mrs. Peacock, are you doing all right? Roy heard what happened last night on his scanner. My goodness, what is the world coming to?" Babs asked as soon as she saw Maggie's landlord. Boy, did the emotions get poured on thick.

"It was horrible. Just horrible. Let me tell you all about it," Mrs. Peacock said as the entire café waited to hear the tale of the attempted home break-in of the Peacock Estate.

Maggie chuckled and thought that might make a good name for a book. Just then, Casper appeared from the back room.

"Good morning, Maggie," he said with a shy grin on his face.

"Hi, Casper. I would have taken the day off if I were you," Maggie said and pushed her glasses up on the bridge of her nose.

"Funny. I was thinking the same thing about you." He nodded his head, making his hair bounce across his forehead.

"I think Joshua said I had to be here no matter what because of the football game. Are you going?" Maggie asked.

She couldn't help but notice the difference already in Casper's demeanor. He looked like he'd ditched a heavy boulder he'd been carrying on his back that only he could feel and see.

"Yeah. I might make an appearance. I'm kind of excited about my new place. You and Babs and Joshua will have to come over when I get it all fixed up."

"Sure. That sounds fun," Maggie replied with an awkward smile. It wasn't that she wouldn't love to see his place. It was just she'd rather look around when no one else was there. Then report back the next day what she thought of it. But there was no reason to worry about a party that wasn't even happening.

"I just wanted to tell you that I'm sorry for the way I talked to you a couple times over the past few days." He stuffed his hands in his pockets. "I didn't know what to say, and you and Joshua had been so nice to me."

Maggie wondered why he thought she was nice to him. She hadn't done anything but order him around and pry into his personal life. If that was being nice, she was afraid to know about his past.

"So, I think the bookshelf for the fancy books you own is finished. If you'd like to take a look, the varnish is dry, and I'm going to attach the glass door. After that, if there is anything you want me to do, I'll be ready," Casper said and flipped his hair to the side, revealing pretty light eyes that looked happy.

"Sure," Maggie said and walked to the back of the store to look at the bookcase. It was beautiful. The wood had transformed from a plain nude color to a rich dark brown that glistened like it was wet even though it was completely dry, hardened, and sealed. It looked like it had been built into the wall with the original design of the building.

"So? Do you like it?" Casper asked.

"It looks… perfect," Maggie said. She nodded and stared at it for a few seconds longer. "Well, the next thing you need to do is put the rare books and the first editions in it. I'll show you where we've been keeping those, and you can arrange them any way you like."

Although she would have liked to handle this herself, there were already people bustling through the store, and she had to get to the register. Poe had found himself the perfect spot for the customers to pass by and give him a steady stream of scratches behind the ears or under his chin.

"Maggie?" Casper stopped her as she tried to walk past. His voice was low and sad.

"Yes?" She looked up at him, squinting.

"I'm sorry. I had to do what I thought was right, and it was hard. I didn't want to get anyone else in trouble. But sometimes that happens. No matter how hard you try," Casper said and extended his hand to her.

Maggie accepted his handshake but was unable to do anything more than smile. He had no idea how bad she felt for snooping and not realizing he was so alone, living out of his car. But she squeezed his hand and cleared her throat before pointing to the high shelves where the collectors' books were stashed.

She let him work by himself, as she guessed he

was a lot like her and preferred to do his tasks alone and without the micromanagement. They were very similar in some ways, but Casper had the courage to do something extraordinary. He was literally helping to make the world better, safer. He'd put himself in danger to do so and kept secrets that could have cost him his life. She thought of her own behavior at Mrs. Peacock's house and how scared she was, how she couldn't move. Yet that old broad was ready to go to war to protect her home and Maggie.

The broken window in the café didn't seem to deter the patrons from lining up like usual. That was another story that Joshua had relayed to Babs and a couple of the regulars who were stationed at their regular seats at the tables and along the bar that lined the wall. It made Maggie slightly uncomfortable when he mentioned that she had come to the shop at that later hour when everything was closed.

A couple of the ladies looked in her direction at the counter in the bookshop, sizing her up as competition. Joshua was still one of the most eligible bachelors in all Fair Haven. The single women hadn't forgotten that in all the hullaballoo over the football game. And the vandalism just caused them to gush and fawn over Joshua even more than they already had been. He seemed to be eating it up this morning, not much different from Mrs. Peacock, who had taken the rest of her story on the road and left the coffee shop with not just Mrs. Donovan in tow but Mrs. Greene and Mrs. Farfarar. They were on the beautification committee in the neighborhood just down the street from Mrs. Peacock. They were all enjoying the drama.

As the morning went on, Maggie watched as female after female asked Joshua if he was all right and if that he needed anything to let them know.

What are you feeling jealous for? You haven't hung your label on him, her conscious taunted.

"But I was at the café when it was vandalized too. And I was at the house where the lunatic who vandalized the café showed up to get the drugs and money he thought I had stolen," Maggie mumbled to Poe, who looked up at her with his glowing eyes, his motor gently humming, making his whole body vibrate.

Even though she had a busy morning and everyone was getting more and more excited as game time approached, Maggie couldn't help but feel she wasn't going to have any fun at this game.

She didn't want to go. What was going to happen, Maggie predicted, would be everyone talking and chatting amongst themselves, and she would be left there sitting slightly away from the crowd, without an inkling as to what was happening on the field. She would be forgotten like the picture she'd painted on the glass that was shattered in a million pieces.

Maggie took a deep breath and noticed one of the books that she had used in her display window. *Coach for a Nation: The Life and Times of Knute Rockne.* She picked it up and looked at the cover. It was an old book, and that was attractive to her immediately. She opened it to chapter one and began to read.

As the customers came and went, with each sale and each question asked, Maggie made it further and further into the book. It wasn't Tolstoy. It was just simply written for everyone to read and enjoy. Suddenly, Maggie wanted to go to the football game. She'd be lost. There was no way to learn the rules and understand everything before she got there. The butterflies in her stomach didn't suddenly disappear. Instead, she read the words that Knute Rockne said: "Courage means being afraid to do something, but still doing it."

She was going to go to this game, and whether she was left alone or not, she was going to enjoy it. She'd make just one pleasant memory for herself, and then she'd be able to look at herself in the mirror and say she was scared but she'd done it.

A chuckle slipped out as she thought of the previous night's shenanigans. She was afraid of Lawrence Tyre getting into the house. But why should going to a football game be scarier than that? Surprisingly, she was enjoying Knute Rockne's story. It didn't solve all of her problems, but it reminded her that everyone had them. She just needed to choose how she handled them.

Just as Maggie was learning about the quote "Win one for the Gipper," Joshua tapped her on the shoulder.

"I think it's about time to get ready for some football." He smiled broadly and winked.

Maggie would have liked to stay and finish her book but remembered what she'd promised herself she was going to do. She was going to go, figure out this stupid game, and have fun. Even if she had to make her own fun. On the sly, she slipped Knute into her purse and figured if nothing else, she'd finish the book before the halfway mark of the game which, she remembered, was called halftime.

"Did I tell you that you are dressed perfectly for a high school football game?" Joshua asked as he locked the door to the bookstore and flipped the closed sign.

"I am?" Maggie looked down at her bulky red sweater and blue jeans. She hadn't paid any attention to what she grabbed this morning. All that was on her mind was being warm and being comfortable. So she broke out her oldest pair of jeans that she usually saved for laundry day and pulled a bulky red sweater she'd found for fifty cents at a thrift store over a couple layers of T-shirts. Her red All-Star gym shoes were a special find she'd been too embarrassed to wear until now. She'd also found a bulldog pin. He was wearing a helmet and had the initials USMC underneath, but she didn't think anyone would mind he wasn't an authentic Fair Haven Bulldog.

"Yup. You look really good," Joshua said as he stood there looking at her as if he were waiting for her to say something else. She blurted out the first thing to come to mind.

"This is a marine pin. I don't think anyone will mind." She pointed awkwardly to the bulldog at her collar like she was a five-year-old doing show-and-tell.

"It's perfect," he replied.

Maggie smiled wide then suddenly remembered who she was smiling at and looked down to tuck her book farther into her purse. She'd bring it back as soon as she finished, and that would be tomorrow, she was sure. But she didn't want Joshua to know she was getting into the spirit of things. Why? She wasn't sure. It was just something she wanted to keep to herself for now and share later with someone who meant the world to her.

Chapter 24

The Fair Haven High School football field was packed. There were families from both teams cheering and laughing and chatting like flocks of seagulls. Cameras were constantly flashing. The band was playing the theme to *Rocky*. The smell of the concession stand was intoxicating, making Maggie's stomach grumble as the thought of gooey nachos and hot dogs crossed her mind.

"Okay, I think I see some room up top." Joshua pointed to a spot that was high up on the bleachers but not the very last row.

"That looks perfect," Babs said with Earl strapped to her belly.

"Now, you be careful, darlin'. Take your time." Roy worried like he always did over her.

"I've got this, honey. You act like I never climbed up a set of bleachers before. We went to high school together. You know I did," she replied as she tugged Earl's little stocking cap over his ears.

"I think I remember you and me under the bleachers a few times," Roy teased, making Babs burst out in flirty giggles.

"Oh, you are bad!" She squealed and kissed him quickly before they ascended the steps.

Joshua sat all the way at the end. Babs and her little family took the seats directly in front of him. Casper filed in next to Joshua. They had obviously formed a bond over the past evening's events, and Maggie was glad for that.

A few rows down, Mrs. Peacock was sitting next to Mrs. Donovan, her arch nemesis, laughing and smiling before she saw Maggie and waved her red-and-blue pom-pom in her direction. Maggie smiled and waved back.

There were several women who approached Joshua again, just like the ones at the café who had asked what happened to the window and touched his arm when they asked if he was okay. Joshua never made it seem like he was interested in any of the ladies, but Maggie couldn't help but feel that familiar twist in her gut of her old friend anxiety coming back to her. She looked around and saw everyone around her talking and waving. Many of the women looked to have gotten dressed up for this event, their hair in long curled waves and makeup done like they would be walking the red carpet later.

But Maggie was determined to sit through the game. She was going to be afraid but go through with it anyway. When the announcer asked everyone to stand for the national anthem, Maggie did, placing her hand over her heart and looking at the field.

This wasn't about her anyway. This was for all the kids on the field. An undefeated season was an amazing accomplishment. She'd heard about there being scouts in the stands and wondered if anyone here was looking for the next Knute Rockne or Walter Payton to pluck from the Fair Haven Bull-dogs and send off to college on a scholarship.

Old Glory waved proudly from on top of the clubhouse. Everyone sang all the words, including Maggie. Once it was over, the crowd clapped wildly. The coin toss was about to take place. Babs was busy talking to Roy, and Roy was busy fussing over

Earl. Casper and Joshua were deep in conversation about something that required they point at the field and make a lot of hand gestures. Maggie felt like a fifth wheel and was about to reach into her purse to pull out her book when she heard a familiar voice.

"I can't believe I was able to spot you in this crowd," Gary said. He was carrying a box filled with nachos, hot dogs, popcorn, and two sodas. Maggie wanted to throw her arms around him and hug him. But instead, she smiled crookedly. She scooted closer to Casper and patted the seat for Gary to sit.

"I thought you'd be too tired for this after last night," Maggie said, unable to stop salivating over the nachos.

"I wasn't going to miss this. Besides, you said you were going to be here. I wasn't going to miss seeing you try to figure out this game," he teased.

"Very funny. I'll have you know, Officer Brookes, that I've been reading up on the subject," Maggie replied, her chin held high as she looked down and pulled out her book to show Gary.

"Are you reading this?"

"Don't act so shocked. I read lots of books." She rolled her eyes. "I work in a bookstore."

"Yeah, but this doesn't seem like anything that would be on your normal list of reading material," Gary said as he scanned the back cover.

"What do you know about it?" She snickered.

"I don't know. You seem more like the *Lady Chatterley's Lover, Fifty Shades of Nonsense* type," Gary said, watching Maggie's eyes bug with surprise.

"I have no interest in reading *Fifty Shades of Nonsense*, thank you. And I read *Lady Chatterley's Lover* and was very disappointed." Maggie huffed, feeling her cheeks get red.

"Not juicy enough for you?" Gary needled, enjoying Maggie's blushing.

"No. It was so boring. Not at all what you'd expect." She shook her head.

"Here, take these. I remember you used to like them in high school." Gary handed her the nachos and one of the soft drinks.

"Thanks. You'll have some too?"

Gary nodded and took a nacho, shoveling it in his mouth. Maggie did the same.

"So, how is the book on Knute Rockne?" Gary asked as the game began and the Bulldogs had the ball first.

"It's pretty good," Maggie said as she started to tell Gary what she'd read so far. They chatted and laughed and cheered for the home team. At half-time, they did the wave with everyone else. Without her noticing, Gary had brought his camera and asked to take a couple pictures of her. Then he got Joshua and Casper in on it. Babs and Roy smiled as Earl slept like an angel in the midst of all the excitement.

Maggie hated to admit it, but she was having a wonderful time. Gary was funny. Joshua and Casper cracked jokes and talked with just about everyone around them. Maggie didn't even seem to mind that the ladies were still going out of their way to talk to Joshua. What did she care? Gary had again saved the day. And by the end of it, the Fair Haven Bull-dogs had won.

About the Author

Harper Lin is a *USA TODAY* bestselling cozy mystery author. When she's not reading or writing mysteries, she loves going to yoga classes, hiking, and hanging out with her family and friends.

For a complete list of her books by series, visit her website.

www.HarperLin.com

www.ingramcontent.com/pod-product-compliance
Lightning Source LLC
Chambersburg PA
CBHW052047240626
47153CB00006B/2250